DOCTOR WHO

TWICE UPON A TIME

Based on the BBC television adventure *Twice Upon A Time* by Steven Moffat

PAUL CORNELL

3 5 7 9 10 8 6 4 2

BBC Books, an imprint of Ebury Publishing
20 Vauxhall Bridge Road,
London SW1V 2SA

BBC Books is part of the Penguin Random House group of companies
whose addresses can be found at global.penguinrandomhouse.com

Doctor Who is a BBC Wales production for BBC One.
Executive producers: Steven Moffat and Brian Minchin

First published by BBC Books in 2018

www.penguin.co.uk

A CIP catalogue record for this book is available from the British Library

ISBN 9781785943300

Editorial Director: Albert DePetrillo
Project Editor: Steve Cole
Cover design: Two Associates
Cover illustration: Anthony Dry
Production: Phil Spencer

Typeset in 11.4/14.6 pt Adobe Caslon Pro
by Integra Software Services Pvt. Ltd, Pondicherry

Printed and bound in Great Britain by Clays Ltd, St Ives PLC

Penguin Random House is committed to a sustainable future for
our business, our readers and our planet. This book is made
from Forest Stewardship Council® certified paper.

Contents

For Tom

'Doctor, I let you go.'

Prologue

Once upon a time, 709 episodes ago, there was an old man who lived in a police box with his friends Ben and Polly. They had many adventures together. But then came one particularly dangerous and exhausting encounter, one that the old man could not survive.

So, in short, he didn't. But there was also a longer version of the story, one that took a long time to be told, one that the old man himself didn't remember, not until right at the end.

But he still ended up living happily ever after.

1

Unexpected Meetings

It was hopeless, to begin with.

Through the snowy emptiness of Antarctica strode a man who was not a man. He wore a long cloak fastened at the neck and a fur hat. Though old, he was still alert and vigorous, and the eyes in his heavily lined face blazed with fierce intelligence. 'No, I can't go through with it,' he was muttering to himself. 'I will fight it. I will not change.'

This was the mysterious traveller in time and space known as the Doctor, and he had just experienced a terrifying encounter with the Cybermen, emotionless silver giants who had tried to invade the Earth. The battle had taken its toll. The Doctor had felt his strength drain from him as the Cybermen's home world, Mondas, had attempted to leech energy from this planet. And he had already pushed his old body to its limits. The Cybermen had finally been foiled by their own cleverness, and he had been little more than a spectator. He had known from his studies of history how the battle would play out, and had blearily watched, making sure that it did, ready to step in, but knowing all the time that, if he stayed, the attack of Mondas would take its toll. So, he had done the right thing, but … but it had not felt like he had done anything much at all, except place a burden around his own shoulders. Once the Cybermen had been defeated, he had quickly headed out here into the emptiness of the Antarctic wastes to find the TARDIS, leaving his two companions, Ben and Polly, rushing to get into their coats, somewhere in the buildings that the snow had already obscured, far behind him. 'It's far from being all over,' that's what he had said to young Ben. And yet … and yet … he somehow could not find the hope he needed to surrender himself and regenerate.

'Hello?' called a voice from in front of him. 'Is someone there?'

The Doctor squinted to try to make out what was ahead. A figure was kneeling in the snow, close to the welcome shape of the blue police box that was the TARDIS. 'Who is that, hmm?'

'I'm the Doctor,' said the mysterious figure.

The Doctor almost laughed at the coincidence. 'Oh, I don't think so! No. Oh dear me, no.' He stepped closer to get a good look at the kneeling man. He was a tall, stark figure, with a shock of silver hair, his features a surprising mixture of joy and sorrow. He was dressed in a black velvet suit and a white shirt, the clothes as tattered and careworn as the man himself seemed to be, and he must surely be on the verge of hypothermia. This was surely some unfortunate survivor of the Cybermen's attack. 'You may be a Doctor, but I am *the* Doctor. The original, you might say!'

This medical man slowly got to his feet, staring at the Doctor in astonishment. He seemed, for a moment, so pleased to see him. '*You!* How can it be you?'

'Do I know you, sir?' There was something about the stranger that felt oddly familiar.

Bizarrely, the man turned to the TARDIS and shouted at it. 'Did you do this? Are you trying to be clever?'

Now the Doctor was sure the man must have been left befuddled by his terrible experiences. Why else would he be addressing what was, for all its miracles, still a mere vehicle? However, there was the possibility that his next move might be to attack it. 'Step away from that machine!'

The stranger seemed suddenly to be lost in thought, continuing to address the blue box. 'No, wait, hang on. Where have you brought me?' He bent to pick up a handful of snow, and, ridiculously, tasted it. 'Oh, minty! This is the South Pole! We're at the South Pole!'

'Well, of course we are!' exclaimed the Doctor, beginning to find this eccentric behaviour extremely tiresome. Here he was, dying, and rather than elegiac grandeur the universe seemed intent on providing him with comic relief. 'Don't you know that?'

The man turned to look at him, those sharp eyes suddenly fixed on him like a predatory bird. 'This is where it happened.'

'Where what happened?'

'This is it, the very first time that I, well … you … *we* regenerated! You're mid-regeneration, aren't you?' He took a step closer and stared even more intently at the Doctor. 'Your face, it's all over the place.' Before the Doctor could protest at these impertinent questions about such personal matters, let alone wonder how he knew so much, the man had grabbed his hand and turned it over to look at his palm. In the very centre of the Doctor's hand was the visible sign of the feeling that had been gripping him for the last few hours, a tiny, sacred, flame of regeneration energy, fluttering in and out of vision. 'You're trying to hold it back.'

The Doctor tore his hand away. The effrontery of this stranger! 'What do you know of regeneration, sir? Are you a Time Lord?'

'You know who I am. You must!'

A terrible fear gripped the Doctor. He couldn't imagine why this man now saw fit to grin at him in that inane matter. He marched over to the TARDIS. 'Have you come to take the ship back?'

The strange individual seemed even more delighted by his words. He skipped over to stand between the Doctor and his vessel, beaming. '"The ship"! You still call it a "ship"!'

But now the Doctor had noticed something even more worrying. 'Dear me, what have you done to it?'

'Nothing.'

The Doctor stepped round his machine, examining it. Why would a Time Lord fix the chameleon circuit, which had been jammed since that landing in London, only to make such trite alterations? 'The colour, it's all wrong! And look at the windows! They're the wrong size!'

Now the man was talking to himself! 'I don't remember this. I don't remember trying not to change. Not back then.'

The Doctor tried to bring the man's attention back to the matter of his TARDIS. 'Look at it! It seems to have ... expanded.'

'Well, all those years of "bigger on the inside", you try sucking your tummy in that long. Why are you trying not to regenerate?'

The Doctor had never taken kindly to being questioned, and the man's tone, both authoritative and foolish at once, was impudent. He drew himself up to his full height. 'Oh, I've never approved of the idea.' Which was true. He had made a point of living on in the same form, even as his body failed him. Some of that was because he had wanted to see his granddaughter, Susan, once again, in this form, as the old man she had loved. That was not all there was to it, of course. But he wasn't about to share truths he had barely acknowledged himself with a complete stranger. 'I have the courage, and the right, to live and die *as myself*.'

'Too late. It's started. A few minutes ago, you were weak as a kitten, right? Now, you're fine. We're in a state of grace, both of us. But it won't last long. We have a choice. Either we change, and go on … or we die as we are.'

The Doctor could tell the stranger knew this process intimately. That he must have regenerated himself, for he obviously was privy to the terrors of it.

Now, however, the man's tone had become fearful: 'But if you … if you die here, if your future never happens, if you don't do the things that you are supposed to do, the consequences could be—' And now he was angry, and the Doctor was about to take enormous umbrage at that, but suddenly the stranger had stopped, halted mid-sentence, as if realising something. 'The snow!'

And indeed, the Doctor could feel it, something had suddenly changed. 'The snow?'

'Look at it!'

The man laid hands on him again, and spun him around, pointing at one of the snowflakes that … was not descending through the air, but hanging there, suspended. As were they all. 'How extraordinary!'

The man reached out a spindly, finely veined hand and flicked the snowflake with his finger. It bobbed away for a moment, then resumed its place. 'Everything's stopped.'

This felt to the Doctor very like something the Time Lords might do. Worryingly so. 'But why?'

'Maybe it's us. Maybe it's something else. But somehow, something has gone very wrong with time!'

2

The Captain

Suddenly, a new voice called out through the suspended blizzard. 'Hello?'

The Doctor turned to see a figure stumbling towards them. The snow swept aside like a curtain to reveal a handsome young man in military uniform. He had a neatly trimmed moustache, and his hair was rather brutally parted. His handsome face had a look of warmth and surprise about it. He had in his hand a pistol, and he was vaguely pointing it in their direction.

What new strangeness was this?

Archie had no idea where he was. He had a vague suspicion this might be the afterlife. However, if it was, it was a deuced unorthodox version of it, and his method of arrival had been decidedly non-traditional also. This felt like neither the Hell he feared or the Heaven he was satisfied that his conduct still deserved.

He had been in the shell crater. That was where things had become strange. Before that, things had been merely terrifying. He and his lads had been laying field telephone cables, one freezing December day, in front-line territory that had been created by a recent barrage, near Saint-Yvon in Belgium. The war against the Germans and their allies had been going less than six months, but already Archie felt that events had bogged down to a degree where it was hard to see how a sudden advance or breakthrough might be achieved. God willing, he had been thinking, the politicians on both sides would see that, and they'd all be going home soon. In the meantime, he was just doing the best he could. That had been what was in his noggin as he heard the terrifying sounds from above, of shells descending. He had shouted to his lads to get into cover. They'd scattered. Someone had yelled something about the Germans breaking through. Archie had been flung off his feet, rolled on landing, and had looked up to find himself staring straight into the face of a German soldier, equally surprised, and equally lost, all on his own, not part of some sudden advance. The chap had handsome, dark features and was clutching his chest; he had a wound of some sort. Archie had gone for his gun and the German had too, and then, both struck by the same dread in the same instant, they had, thank God, both hesitated. They had lain there, weapons aimed at each other. After a few moments, Archie had decided to attempt conversation.

'There is something I should like to say. That is, there is something I should very much like you to understand. I do not have the slightest desire to kill you.' The man had given no sign of comprehending him, but Archie had soldiered on. 'The only possible reason I would do so would be self-defence. However, since you are *aware* I might kill you in self-defence, there is the strong possibility *you* will kill *me* in self-defence, before *I* can kill *you* in self-defence.' Archie had doubted his classical ethics prep was getting through to the man, but he had to say something. 'But that's what this whole shooting match is about, really, isn't it? Who kills whom in self-defence first. God must look down and laugh, don't you think? Or weep. I think weep.' And there it had been, he had gone from attempting some civil distance to desperately trying to find fellow-feeling in this equally terrified stranger. The German had remained obstinately silent. 'Does rather make me wish that you understood English,' Archie had said, finally.

'*Bitte,*' said the German, '*hau ab! Lass mich einfach hier. Ich will dich nicht töten bitte geh.*'

Which had *sounded* plaintive. 'Or that I spoke German,' Archie had admitted. 'War is hell, eh?'

Which was, ominously, given his present situation, the exact moment that the strangeness had begun. There had been the sound of another shell descending, far too close. Right above them. He had had that sudden sickening sensation in his stomach that here came death, from a new direction. But then he had felt a weird stillness to the air. He had realised that the German's gun, which had been shaking in his hands, had ceased to do so. The man's face had frozen into immobility. Archie had looked closer and found, to his astonishment, that a single bead of perspiration, detached from the man's nose, was hanging in the air, caught in the moment of falling.

Was this a miracle? He had always wanted to be present for one of those. Carefully, keeping his gun on the German, he had gotten to his feet. Then he had seized his chance to scarper. He had scrambled quickly out of the shell crater, with the intent of finding as many of his lads as possible, and dragging them, if he had to, back to the British trenches. He'd stopped for a moment to take in the vision before him. For the first time in his experience, the battlefield was silent. The plains of war stretched endlessly, explosions frozen like flowers in the distance. A single bird hung in the air, its wings motionless. Small fires all around were like stilled depictions of flame. He had been startled to see how close his lads were, in a nearby shell hole. They had, of course, got a brew on. One of them had lifted his mug halfway to his lips. Archie had never felt so lost, and yet inspired. He felt hope to see all this, as well as terrible fear. It had been like looking at an oil painting of his life. He had turned, staring at the beautiful horror of it all.

He had turned to see, standing there, the woman made of glass.

What was a statue doing here? That's what he'd thought. Perhaps he had simply gone cuckoo. About time, if so. Quite a relief, actually, that it had turned out to be this entertaining. The statue had its back to him. He had approached it, wondering at such a fragile thing remaining intact, wondering if perhaps the battle had stopped in order for it to do so.

Which was when the statue had turned and looked at him.

She had raised her hand, and for a moment Archie, though terrified, had been sure that here was some divine visitation, who had put a halt to the horrors of war, and was about to take him home to the poppy fields of East Anglia. Then he was somehow somewhere else, somewhere he had just a moment to glimpse was a sort of giant stone chamber. He had struggled to fit that into any belief system, but then, a moment later, he had fallen sidelong, it had felt, into a white room, something like an operating theatre. It had felt like something was going wrong, as if something had somehow struck him and sent him off course. He had had another moment to react in horror at the white room, when suddenly all around him had become red, lights flashing into his eyes and mind, and a calm lady's voice repeating, 'Timeline error, there is a timeline error.'

Then blackness.

He had awoken, if that process could be called waking, because he was pretty sure that hadn't been a dream, with his back on snow. He had heaved himself up, expecting to be either once again in the fields of war, or in one of the strange worlds he had glimpsed. But he was in neither. He was freezing even more than he had been, the chill around him terrifying in its intensity. He had quickly started to move, feeling that this cold would cut him down in moments. He had never felt a cold like it. And yet the landscape seemed like something one might expect in … Norway? Iceland? Was he perhaps at one of the poles? Except … the snow was literally hanging in the air, just as the explosions had been frozen on his battlefield. Fortunately, he had quickly seen lights ahead, had heard voices, and they had been speaking English!

He had hailed the two figures he saw ahead. Now he saw them turn to watch his approach. 'Sorry. So sorry,' he said as he reached them. He now felt sure he must have had a head wound, hence all his absurd thoughts about the afterlife, for these were no angels. He had perhaps returned to his right frame of mind having wandered to a different part of the battlefield. A very different part. 'I don't suppose either of you is a doctor?'

The two figures looked at each other, then back to him. 'Are you trying to be funny?' the taller one said. It seemed from his accent that he shared Archie's Scottish heritage.

Archie put a hand to his head. What did that mean? What did any of this mean? Suddenly, an impossible white light was shining over the three of them. It came from behind him. It spoke of pursuit. He spun around, and found himself backing away, past the two strangers, who, courageously or ignorantly, stayed there, facing the threat, looking, somehow, directly at the light that was blinding him. 'She's coming!' he whispered. 'She's coming! It's her!' The reaction of these two gentlemen was astonishing. They visibly steeled themselves, the taller one adjusting his cuffs, the shorter one grasping his lapels. He wanted to yell at them that what was coming was beyond his understanding, but, hang on, so were they, and there was something terribly reassuring about what they were doing. But here she was, that terrifying figure, looming out of the light. Surely they would panic now? Surely they would turn and run?

'Not human, I think,' said the fellow in the fur hat, 'but not a Cyberman either.'

'Oh, of course,' said the Scottish one, 'you've just been fighting Cybermen too.' He glanced past Archie, who turned to see that standing there was … a police box, that was what his Glaswegian friends had told him they were called, when he'd popped up there for the family reunion. Only this one was ultra-modern in looks, bang up to date. Ah, the Scotsman must have brought it with him for some reason. Oddly, the tall dandy was now addressing the box, as if there was someone watching from inside. 'Having fun with the parallels, dear?' Had the Scotsman brought his wife with him as well as his police box? He must have a hell of a big sleigh.

But the old chap in the furry hat was now calling out to the glass woman, who had slowed her approach, perhaps as puzzled by these newcomers as Archie was. 'Kindly identify yourself! If you are not from this world, state your planet of origin and your intentions. This is Earth, a level five civilisation!'

'And it is protected!' snarled the Scotsman.

Oh. Were these gentlemen perhaps Martians? So … Martian, Scotsman, police box, wife, sleigh … ? Archie decided he should probably stop trying to construct any sort of working hypothesis and just be glad these chaps seemed to be on his side.

'It's what?' asked the one in the hat. 'Protected?'

To Archie's immense relief, the light snapped off and the glass woman vanished.

'Oh,' said the Scot, 'Okay. That usually doesn't work.'

'Protected by whom?' the Englishman persisted.

'Oh, it *is* early days, isn't it?'

'Well, whatever that thing was, it's still around. The snow, you see. Still frozen.' The Englishman indicated the suspended snowflakes.

'Yes, I think you're probably right.'

Archie jumped as the two of them suddenly rounded on him. 'Sir,' said the Englishman, 'that creature, what is it, and what does it want with you?'

'I don't know. I don't even know what I'm doing here.' Still, it was only fair to warn them. 'But it's me it's after. You'll find me dangerous company.'

The Englishman chuckled. 'I flatter myself you'll find me the same! May I suggest, for your own safety, you step on board my ship?'

Archie looked around. 'What ship?'

'He means,' said the Scotsman, with a worrying twinkle in his eye, 'get inside the box.'

3

Inside the Box

The Doctor, now in his twelfth incarnation, had no idea how he had got here, but he had to admit, in what felt like some strange release from where he had been ... he was enjoying himself. The last thing he had known, he'd been on the battlefield, and had managed to get the remaining Cybermen close enough to ... well, to sacrifice himself to save others. He had known that was going to be the case when he had set out that day. His only regret had been that his friend Bill – his lost, blameless friend Bill – had decided to share in his sacrifice. That she should have been put in that position, where that was the best result. He recalled the tremendous violence of the explosion, then somehow waking in the TARDIS, which had been in flight. He must have staggered from the scene, he thought, somehow managed to hit the controls. But ... what a strange choice for the old girl to have brought him here. He had, in those few moments before he had glimpsed his other self, decided upon something, something very serious. It was, in some ways, a continuation of a decision made before he had set out to confront the Cybermen. That decision had set him free to laugh again.

It was a decision that meant he no longer had to bear the pain of hope.

He had only the slightest of theories as to why time had then stopped, that perhaps it had something to do with the TARDIS's odd decision that he should run into his former self. He had equally little idea how this soldier had got here, but he was deeply in love with the concept of what was about to happen right at this moment. This was the sort of comedy he was free to enjoy now, right at the end.

The First Doctor had taken out his ancient key and was unlocking the door to the TARDIS. 'It may,' he was saying, like a magician about to astound his audience, 'look a little snug from this angle, but I think you might be in for a—'

The Doctor quickly stepped forward to follow them both inside. He had just about resisted skipping. He joined the other two inside the console room of *his* TARDIS. The First Doctor was standing there, struck dumb by, well, a million brilliant design choices, all of them far beyond the old man's comprehension.

'My TARDIS!' the old boy finally exclaimed. 'Look at my TARDIS!'

'This is impossible!' To add to the delight, the soldier was doing the standard double-take.

'Have I been burgled?' gasped the First Doctor.

The Doctor frowned.

'It's …' began the soldier, 'but it's …' Glorious? Awe-inspiring? *Tasteful?*

'Hideous,' finished the First Doctor.

'Bigger on the inside than it is on the outside,' finished the soldier, more aptly.

The Doctor quickly closed the doors behind them. 'You know, I thought it probably was. Glad it's not just me.' Still, the First Doctor's lack of basic design sense had dented his mood a little.

'What is this place?' asked the soldier.

'This place,' said the First Doctor, 'is, or ought to be, my TARDIS!'

The Doctor decided to put the old man out of his misery. He bounded over to the console, brought up a live feed from outside, and spun the monitor into the First Doctor's eye line. Another police box stood in the snow. The one in which he, as the First Doctor, had arrived all those millennia ago. 'Technically, *that* is your TARDIS. It's about seventy feet that way.' He pointed. 'See? Always remember where you parked. It's going to come up a lot.'

The soldier, meanwhile, was still gazing at his surroundings, utterly lost. 'Is this madness? Am I going mad?'

'Madness?' The Doctor felt he had best be blunt with the man. It'd give him a chance to find his footing.

Directness and honesty were always the best policies. That was something he had always been certain about in this incarnation. 'Well, you're an officer from World War One, at the South Pole, being pursued by an alien through frozen time. Madness was never this good.'

'World War One?'

The Doctor had realised that the First Doctor was making a slow perambulation around the console. He'd become distracted by the possibility that the old man, overwhelmed by the quality of the dashboard, might fiddle with something. But now he glanced back to the soldier for a moment. 'Judging by the uniform, yes.'

'Yes, but ... what do you mean ... *One*?'

Ah. The Doctor slowly turned back to the man, wincing at how he'd just trod on a butterfly there. Directness and honesty, he kept being reminded in this incarnation, were only *sometimes* the best policies. The soldier was now looking at him as if all the terrors of Earth's history had suddenly been made real and immediate for him. What would the Doctor's wife, River Song, say in these circumstances? She'd had a handy phrase, hadn't she, for when horrors intruded on the dinner party? He remembered. 'Oh, sorry ... spoilers.'

'Enough of this!' called the First Doctor. 'Who are you?'

The Doctor was relieved to let the ... Captain—yes, that was the man's rank—withdraw to consider. He turned to his former self, with no more appetite for pretence. 'You know who I am. You knew the moment you saw me. I'd say, "Stop being an idiot," but I kind of know what's coming.' He couldn't resist a little smirk at his own cleverness. His current cleverness, that was. Surely the penny was about to drop?

'I assure you,' the First Doctor said, dropping his cloak into the Doctor's hands as if he were a bellboy, 'I do not have the faintest idea who you are.'

The Doctor dumped the cloak on a chair. 'Well, I know who *you* are.'

The Captain, meanwhile, had been rifling through, of all things, the video cabinet. 'Is anyone going to explain what's going on?' he asked, holding up a VHS cassette on which the Doctor could just make out ... ah, that was his recording of the Daleks' master plan. They'd dearly love to get that back, having lost their own copy centuries ago.

Enough was enough. The Doctor strode up to his former self and held up his palm to show him the light that burned there. 'Snap.'

There we go. Finally. The old man reacted in horror. 'You ... are me? No. No!'

'Yes. Yes, I'm very much afraid so.' And he couldn't make a joke out of it any more. There was the horror again. The horror they were both facing individually, and, oddly, together.

'Do I become ... you?'

'Well, there's a few false starts.' The Doctor grinned. 'But you get there in the end.'

'But I thought ...?'

'What?'

'Well, I *assumed* I'd ... get ...' The First Doctor suddenly seemed to decide that the best course of action would be to turn his confusion into something rather more pointed. '*Younger.*'

'I *am* younger!'

The Doctor only had a moment to regret that that had come out as a sort of anguished howl before the Captain stumbled back towards the console. He was holding a hand to his head. 'You know, I really don't think I'm completely following ... Oh dear.' He looked like he was about to collapse at any moment.

'Oh, you poor fellow,' said the First Doctor, 'you're in shock. Let me help you.' He led the soldier to sit down on the steps that led to the upper deck. 'Brandy,' he ordered grandly, as if about to snap his fingers for service. 'Get him brandy! Do you have any? I had a bottle somewhere.'

'Hang on!' The Doctor dashed over to the drinks cabinet.

'Now you sit here, my boy, collect your wits.'

'Who *are* you people?' asked the Captain.

'I am the Doctor, and this is my, umm ...'

The Doctor arrived back with a bottle of the Aldebaran brandy that River had liked so much, one that bad been buried at the back of the cabinet for … well, it probably wasn't even one of hers. He was considering what would be the best policy here. Directness and honesty were always … no, perhaps not. 'It's complicated. Actually *I* am also—'

'My nurse,' finished the First Doctor, with a twinkle.

'Excuse me?'

'I realise that seems a little improbable—'

'Well, yes—' The Doctor wasn't looking forward to having to play along with this.

'—because he's a man,' finished the First Doctor. The Captain nodded in agreement.

'*What*?!'

'Older gentlemen, like women, can be put to use.'

'You … you can't say things like that!' For goodness' sake, this was like Christmas dinner on Gallifrey. What about Barbara, the Doctor wanted to yell. She was one of your greatest friends, brilliant in every way, and she wouldn't have stood for a statement like that. What, is this you acting up because we've got company?

'Can't I?' grumped the First Doctor. 'Says who?'

'Just about everyone you're going to meet for the rest of your life.' He shoved the bottle in the First Doctor's direction. 'Here.'

The First Doctor took the bottle and examined it. The Doctor realised, to his annoyance, that there was a mark on the side, one that he had put there and forgotten about. But the old coot obviously hadn't. 'Hmm. Have you had some of this?'

'Well, you know,' hissed the Doctor, 'I may have snuck a glass at some point in the last fifteen hundred years. It's been rock and roll.'

The First Doctor made a high-pitched noise of disapproval and poured a glass for the Captain. 'There you are, get this down you, and you'll feel a lot better.'

The Captain did so, looking thankful for both the liquor and the familiarity of the experience. 'Thank you, yes.'

The First Doctor looked back to the Doctor, clearly troubled. 'I don't understand any of this.'

'Of course you understand. I am your future self.'

'Are you indeed? And I suppose this is meant to be my TARDIS?'

'*Our* TARDIS.' Now, *there* was diplomacy his wife would have approved of.

'What's wrong with the lights?'

'The lights?'

'Yes, why don't you turn the lights on?'

The Doctor recalled that the First Doctor hadn't had the experience to change his TARDIS interior from factory settings. He must have gotten used to that brutalist glare. Which, of course, he'd then cluttered up with those so-called antiques he'd got from jumble sales. 'The lights *are* on. It's supposed to be like this.'

'Why?'

By the Rivers of Rassilon, the old man always had made a thing of the pointed question, hadn't he? 'I don't know, it's … atmospheric.'

'Atmospheric?' The First Doctor bristled. 'This is the flight deck of the most powerful space-time machine in the known universe—not a restaurant for the French!'

The most powerful? The Doctor couldn't believe the cheek of the old man. He wasn't talking to one of his ape hostages now! But his former self had gone to look at … Oh dear.

He was pointing at the Doctor's beloved Yamaha SGV 800, placed carefully on its stand. 'Good Lord, what is that?'

The Doctor winced. 'Oh,' he said, 'look what someone must have accidentally left there.'

The Captain perked up at once more recognising something familiar. 'I say, it's some sort of guitar, isn't it?'

'Oh,' coughed the Doctor, 'is it yours?'

The First Doctor wandered over to peer closely at the instrument, like it was one of his antiques. 'It appears to have been played quite recently.' The Doctor remembered his former self's pretensions to being the Time Lord answer to Sherlock Holmes. 'It's the only thing here that's been cleaned.' He went over to the console, wiped a finger along it and held it up. His gloved finger had perhaps got slightly dirtier. 'In fact, this whole place is in need of a good dusting.

Obviously,' the great detective deduced, 'Polly isn't around any more.'

He's doing this just to make me feel awkward, isn't he? Isn't he? 'Please, please ... *please* stop saying things like that.'

Which was, awkwardly, the moment the Doctor heard a woman's voice ring out through the TARDIS. It was clear, cool, eerily serene. 'Doctor?' it said.

The effect on the Captain was immediate. He looked around in panic once more. 'That voice, I've heard it before!'

'Am I addressing the Doctor?' asked the voice.

The Doctors looked at each other. The Doctor decided he really should let the old man have a go at this. You know, give the intern a bit of on-the-job experience. He indicated that the First Doctor should proceed. The First Doctor grudgingly accepted his gallantry and turned to the direction the voice seemed to be coming from. 'Doctor who?'

The Doctor had to smile. How many times had that been asked of him?

'You are a Time Lord from the planet Gallifrey,' the voice said. 'You travel in a Type 40 TARDIS, with a defective cloaking mechanism. You formerly belonged to the Prydonian chapter, but have renounced your vows.'

The First Doctor glanced back to him, worried. Whoever this was, they were very well informed.

Which must come as more of a surprise to the old man, who'd kept his every move a secret. 'Clearly, you have done some elementary research,' said the First Doctor, turning back to the voice. 'Am I supposed to be impressed, hmm?'

'Your title of choice is "Doctor", however your real name is—'

'Yes, yes,' muttered the First Doctor, 'well, that's quite enough of that.' The Doctors shared a look of alarm. She knew the name. That was the sign of a serious player. 'You have the advantage of me, madam.'

The Doctor went to the console, and ran his fingers over the scan controls, sending sensor waves throughout the ship and outside it, attempting to discover the nature of the threat. There came a sudden, enormous noise of impact. The Doctor was thrown from his feet. Something was smashing against the TARDIS!

4

Confrontations

The Doctor hauled himself upright. That impact had sounded from close by the doors. And now a second concussion rang out, this one striking from the other direction. The First Doctor and the Captain were stumbling to and fro. But this was extraordinary. Nothing could attack the TARDIS like this. Nothing that didn't have tremendous cosmic powers.

'What is that? What are you doing?' the First Doctor was shouting. To him this must have been even more extraordinary. His 'ship' had been inviolate. 'What is happening?'

The look on the Captain's face said he was sure the terrible spirit that was pursuing him was knocking on the door; that his sanctuary was about to be breached.

There came another impact, then another, at the remaining cardinal points. So, wait a second, there'd been one on each of the four corners of the ship, right? A moment later, the Doctor's suspicion was confirmed, as, impossibly, overriding every setting of the interior geography, the room around them lost its moorings and began to sway. It was as if … as if …

The Doctor leapt across the rolling deck, grabbed the doors and flung them open. The freezing air rushed in, the suspended snow remaining stock still within it. The Doctor looked out, and found himself looking down on the tiny lights of Snowcap Base, where he had fought the Cybermen, and at the tiny shape of the First Doctor's TARDIS beside it. His own TARDIS had indeed been lifted up into the air, and they were already dangling hundreds of feet above the ground. Those impacts, the swaying, might just have been the old girl's direct way of letting him know what was going on. Or perhaps whatever this was really did have the power to invade his space like this.

Beside the doorway was the end of a grimy metal clamp, blackened and ancient, attached to the corner of the TARDIS. He clambered up and looked around the ship. On each corner there was a similar clamp. He looked up. A cable attached the clamps to a vast spaceship of a very strange design. It was like an enormous stone castle, floating in the sky. If time hadn't been halted, the guys down on Snowcap Base would have been wondering if this was the work of more Cybermen.

As the Doctor watched, an iris opened in the base of the ship. The cable began to be retracted. They were being hauled in. This was, the Doctor thought, the story of his life. If it wasn't one thing, it was another.

He ducked back inside. The old man was clinging to the console, and still shouting in the direction the voice had come from. 'Where are you taking us, hmm?' There was silence. 'Hello there?' Beside him stood the Captain, clearly dumbfounded but doing his best to be brave.

The Doctor closed the doors. 'She's hung up.'

'Well,' the First Doctor slapped his hands together. 'Time we were off, then.' He made to move around the console, reached out a hand, his fingers fidgeting … and found that what he was reaching for wasn't there. 'You've moved everything!'

The Doctor reached the console and swiftly hit his own lift-off sequence. The ship began to wheeze and groan and … shut down with a clunk. 'Can't start the engines. Some kind of signal, blocking the command path.'

'How could they possibly have the knowledge?' asked the First Doctor.

'They know our *name*.'

With a clang from outside, the TARDIS ceased to sway. They had been placed back down on something solid. Doubtless the floor of the spaceship had sealed beneath them. They all turned to look at the doors.

Whatever power could do this, thought the Doctor, might well have the knowledge to enter the ship without his permission.

But this time, diplomatically almost, when the voice called it called from outside. 'Exit your capsule. The Chamber of the Dead awaits you.'

What to do? The Doctor looked to his other self. This time, the old man seemed willing to let him take the lead. The Doctor lowered his voice. 'Obviously, we have one little advantage.'

'What advantage?' asked the First Doctor. 'Whoever these creatures are, they know everything about us.'

'Not everything. They don't know there's two of us.' The First Doctor smiled impishly at that idea and patted him on the arm.

The Doctor wasn't sure he liked being touched by his other self. Apart from the awkward intimacy of it, Time Lords tended not to get touchy-feely with their previous incarnations. It just wasn't done, because, in most circumstances, it would cause a shorting out of the time differential as the Blinovitch Limitation Effect came into play. In short: zap. Clearly, whatever had happened to time, it was shutting off that effect too. His earlier self should know that full well, he'd already had a lot of experience with ... but then the Doctor noticed the First Doctor examining his glove where he'd patted the Doctor, and realised that actually the old boy had come to the right conclusion before he had. 'If they think you're out there talking to them,' he continued, 'they won't think you're also in here, getting the engines back on line.'

The First Doctor considered for a moment, looking rather taken aback. 'Of course,' he admitted. 'Very good. I should have thought of that.'

'You will, Doctor. You will.' The Doctor grinned; the old boy wanted to be in charge, of course. All the other selves he'd met had taken pity on the youth and let him, but he wouldn't get his own way with *this* incarnation! He slammed down the security controls. 'Field's up.'

The First Doctor nodded, adjusted his cravat and straightened his waistcoat. He was ready for action. The Captain looked awkwardly between them, a grateful expression on his face, as if he was feeling unworthy of all this protection.

The Doctor watched his earlier self march towards the doors, clutching his lapels, and felt at once nostalgia for how brave he'd once been, and nervousness at how that bravery had in part been born of sheer ignorance. 'Come on,' he whispered to the Captain. 'Let's get to work.'

The First Doctor had not been having a very good day. For one thing, he was desperately trying to hold his form, his very personality, together, against the great and terrible change he had worked so hard to avoid. That was taking a large portion of his mental powers. On top of that, he'd found himself dealing with that old fogey, his own personal, and very worrying, Ghost of Christmas Future. For Scrooge, that spectre had been the ghost of his own death. In his case it merely meant several things of which he very much disapproved, including nonsense, frippery, and seemingly not being in possession of a comb. Still, he was about to do what he did best. He was about to look something terrifying in the eye and indicate to it that he really didn't think it was up to much. Not compared to him. Doing that would be just the tonic he needed at the moment.

He stepped out of the wastrel's TARDIS into an enormous chamber, carved, seemingly, from stone. It took the form of a cylinder, winding up above him to a vanishing point in the darkness. It was lined with alcoves, each about the size of a person, as if this were some sort of tomb. The TARDIS stood in its very centre, the four clamps still attached to it, the cable vanishing into the space above. The floor was an iris, which, having admitted them, was closed now.

He appeared to be alone. The most prominent feature of the chamber was a stone staircase, of the sort that traditionally led to a throne, designed to put awe into everyday people. Hmm, then it was good that he was not so everyday! A bright light was shining from the top of that staircase. Obviously. As if this were some deity he was approaching, and he was not to observe the face of the god. Such theatre! He took a few paces forward, to the point he remembered from the design specifications of his own ship. He hoped that the old fogey had made what he was measuring out work correctly, like he'd fixed everything else.

'Look around you,' the calm female voice said. 'You stand in the Chamber of the Dead. You are known to all here.'

Now, that was more like it. He scraped a line on the floor with the heel of his shoe, describing a portion of an arc around the ship. 'The TARDIS has a force field around it. It extends this far. I may cross, but you may not.' Well, hopefully not with more than her projected voice, anyway. For all the First Doctor knew, this was sheer bluff, but sheer bluff was his second language. As he was about to demonstrate. 'Any attempt to enter my ship will, I promise you, fail.'

'Your caution is well advised.'

Who did she think she was talking to? Well, obviously, she knew exactly who she was talking to, but even so … The First Doctor held back his emotions and came out with a chuckle. 'Oh, I've never liked that word.'

'What word?'

'Caution.' With that, he completed the second part of the plan he had had in mind as he left the ship. He stepped across the line. 'Please do not make the mistake of assuming I am in any way afraid of you. I am an old man. At my time of life, there is nothing left to fear, hmm?'

Inside the TARDIS, the Doctor was working on the engines with both hands, up to his elbows in circuitry, while keeping one eye, via the monitor, on what the First Doctor was getting up to outside. 'Oh,' he whispered, 'just you wait!'

'We do not expect your fear,' said the voice. 'We know who you are.'

'Yes, so you've been making clear.' The First Doctor was waiting for the woman to become affronted by his impudence and reveal some information about herself. But that blasted calmness of hers was going to take some chipping away at.

'The Bringer of Darkness. The Imp of the Pandorica. The Beast of Trenzalore.'

Was it possible she actually *did* have him confused with someone else? 'No, no, dear me, no. I am the Doctor.'

'You are the Doctor of War.'

Now he was certain she was making it up. Regeneration might cause him to become the elderly fop he had just met, a dandy or a clown or a schoolboy, but it would never befoul his essential nature. He began to chuckle. Madam, he thought to himself, you should never bluff an old bluffer.

Inside the TARDIS, Archie had been watching the face of the Doctor with an increasing wariness. He had ceased his important work on his machine, work that Archie had realised was intimately connected with escaping their predicament and saving Archie's own skin, in order to watch the amazing wireless pictures of what was transpiring outside. What that dratted woman was saying to the English Doctor seemed to be disquieting the Scottish one terribly. This man bore burdens, Archie realised, that he had seldom seen on mortal shoulders. But above all there was guilt. A guilt that had been fought off, bargained with, overcome, perhaps, but a guilt that sprung eternal. He had perhaps lost someone, very recently, Archie thought. This expression was one he had only previously seen on the faces of those that had seen death. And, he shuddered to think of it, on the faces of the dying.

'The Doctor, yes,' said the First Doctor, 'but the "Doctor of War"?' He rose to his full height, clutching his lapels in magnificent certainty. 'Never, madam. Never.'

'We will not fight the Doctor of War. Instead, we offer you a gift.'

Ah, now this was more like it. Whether this reputation was deserved or not, it had bought him some respect, and, more importantly, it had bought the Doctor inside the TARDIS time. 'What gift?'

'Return to us the human on your TARDIS, and in exchange, you may speak with her again.'

The First Doctor frowned. He had a tiny, profound hope in his heart, that perhaps, if it turned out this powerful being really did know who he was, beyond all this 'war' nonsense, then perhaps … perhaps she was referring to his granddaughter? They had had a much better second parting, in the end. He had had a few hours to meet her family. But, at this moment of all moments, to see her again, that would be a joy. 'Speak with *whom*?'

A beam of light shot out from one of the alcoves at floor level. The light formed into a tunnel, and down it moved a shadow. Someone was approaching down this corridor. The First Doctor steeled himself for disappointment. Then he saw the face of this stranger and felt it nevertheless, like a slow blade to his heart.

Archie saw the Doctor leap up from the console. He stared at the monitor in shocked disbelief. The expression of loss on his face had suddenly been replaced with the most curious and frightening mixture of hope and … fury.

Before Archie could say anything, all important tasks forgotten, and without a word, the Doctor ran for the doors.

5

Cats and Space Adventures

Bill Potts had no idea how she'd gotten here. Nor did she know where 'here' was. Nor did she have a clue who the old man was in front of her. Grandpa was looking at her like she was an unwanted Christmas present. 'Young lady,' he said, in a voice made for selling life insurance to the over-fifties, 'who are you?'

And then she saw. Behind him, just standing there, was the amazing thing she'd first seen in a tutor's office at university, the object which had turned out to be escape and adventure and horror and joy and life and death and then a bit more, thank God. The TARDIS. Which meant ... 'Is he here? Is the Doctor here?' She realised she hadn't remembered to breathe and solved that with a quick gulp of air. 'Oh my God, is he *alive*?'

Which was when the doors flew open and the Doctor ran out. And oh, the look on his face.

'Doctor!' she yelled. She ran to him, she ran to him without another thought in her head and she threw her arms around him. 'I knew it! I did, I knew it! I knew you couldn't stay dead, you don't have the concentration.' She was grinning up at him, waiting to get the normal rise out of him she'd come to love, the one that said Bill and the Doctor were back, that the whole universe was again theirs to explore. But that wasn't the look he was giving her. He was, in fact, gently detaching himself from her. He was being deliberately distant and cold. Oh, don't do this to me again, you idiot. 'Doctor?' He took his sonic screwdriver from his coat. 'Doctor, what are you doing?'

'Please,' he said, and there was his voice, gentle and careful, 'just keep still.'

He scanned her with the screwdriver, running it up and down in front of her, listening to its changing tone. What the hell? Did he think she was infected or something? Oh, she got it now. And yeah, okay, this was something he'd probably learned to check for before he did the hugging, probably something that happened quite a lot, the alien duplicate thing. Like with those Zygon things he'd shown her in what he'd called his 'intelligent species who are just a bit different from us' book, but which had had 'monster book' on the cover. It was kind of irritating to be on the receiving end, though.

'Doctor, stop that, it's me.'

Suddenly, the Doctor was looking at her. 'Bill Potts.' It was like her name hurt him just on its own. She realised why. The last time he'd seen her ... 'My *friend*

Bill Potts was turned into a Cyberman. She gave her life to save a lot of people she barely knew. So let's be clear: nobody *imitates* Bill Potts. Nobody *mocks* Bill Potts.'

Which so made her want to cry, but no, she couldn't have this, couldn't let him feel this pain a moment longer. 'Bill Potts is standing right in front of you.'

'How? How is that even possible?'

She let herself grin her biggest grin, the one she'd loved to show him when they'd faced down the horrors together. 'Well ... long story short, I totally pulled.'

'You did *what*?' said Grandpa.

'Heather, do you remember? The girl in the puddle?' Which was an offhand way to describe a living space-time craft, who was also a real, complete person, gorgeous and loving and ... stuff. 'She showed up, she came for me.' It had been on the battlefield, with Cybermen falling all around. Bill herself had fallen, and that was the last time the Doctor would have seen her, seemingly dead, and not even dead as herself. But then Heather had appeared, from outside of space and time, and used her power to manipulate the construction of ... everything. She had taken the information that was Bill, and had made her a new body, constructed of the same miracles that Heather was. They had returned the unconscious Doctor to his TARDIS, and left him there. It had been the best they could do; Heather had found the body of a Time Lord beyond her power to heal. And yet they'd both felt there had still been a spark of something in him, something that just needed time to rest. Then they'd left to explore. Was that why he was looking at her so coldly now? Should they have tried harder to find him, to check up on him?

They'd had a look around the Milky Way, checked out everything Bill had ever wanted to see that the Doctor hadn't already shown her, and all that time Bill had been working Heather out, trying to figure out if this was a relationship, or just friends with *serious* benefits, or what. She'd asked, in the end, as they stood on the surface of Pluto, watching its moons set, if they could try Earth for a bit, if she could go back to being human, and if maybe Heather wanted to try it again too? Except not if it was a one-way deal, because she never wanted to give this up. Heather had said sure, they could give it a go. So they'd had Christmas, back being flesh and blood, going out clubbing, magicking up enough money to put down a deposit on a flat, staying up late to watch old movies. Bill had discovered, kind of at the same time Heather had, Heather as a real person. And she'd become a real person that she'd fallen in love with.

But the Doctor had that terrible look on his face again. 'She came to rescue you, did she?'

'Yeah, she did.'

'How romantic. Where is she?'

Bill wanted to come out with a snappy comeback, but now she thought about it ... she was certain, somehow, that she'd had her happy ending, that she and Heather had lived a long and really kind of exciting life together, with cats and space adventures, but how could that be true when here she was, not much older than when she'd left the Doctor? 'Well, she's … she's …' Everything after that first Christmas with Heather felt cloudy, like it hadn't happened yet, but somehow she knew that it would. She didn't feel like she had her special space powers, either. What the hell was going on here?

'Come on, where is she? Where's Heather, and how did you get here?'

'I … I don't … I can't …'

He checked the readings on his sonic screwdriver. 'You can't remember. No, I bet you can't.' He stalked around her, still scanning her.

Meanwhile, Grandpa had wandered over, and was looking at them with one eyebrow as high as she'd ever seen an eyebrow go. 'That device; what is it?'

'Sonic screwdriver.'

'A *what* screwdriver?'

'Really,' said the Doctor, ignoring him, 'it's a very good job.'

'I'm sorry,' interrupted Grandpa, 'an *audio* screwdriver?'

'There are only three low-key markers indicating that she's a duplicate.'

'I'm not a duplicate!' Bill found she was pleading with him. Because this was painful. Whatever he was picking up, it was about Heather space stuff, right? Right?

'Could easily have missed them. Hard to be analytical, when you have so much … hope.' And he shared a moment there with Grandpa, who had been looking between them with considerably more compassion on his face. 'What was it old Borusa used to say at the Academy? "In hope, you are at your weakest."'

Grandpa looked angry at him. Which was exactly right as far as Bill was concerned.

The Doctor turned towards the stairs and called up to the top. 'So! You! You who gave me hope and took it away! Who are you? Who has been stealing the faces of the dead?' He started to ascend the stairs.

Bill was furious at him, but she also couldn't really blame him. How many times had he seen his friends transformed, herself included? Who would want to inflict such cruelty on the Doctor? 'Doctor, want me with you?' And that hadn't come out all brave and heroic like she'd meant it to, demonstrating that this was the real her, but actually … bit whiny.

He looked back to her. There was such pain on his face. 'I would like that more than anything in the world. But, Bill … I'm sorry … you're not here.' And he kept walking.

Bill stared after him. Well, that hurt. That hurt like … death, all over again.

After a moment of looking between them like a startled parrot, Grandpa came bustling over. 'Oh my dear, I am so sorry about his behaviour.' The look in his eyes was such a relief. This old man was sure about his moral compass, and he didn't seem to care who or what she was. 'Well,' he continued, '*my* behaviour. In advance.'

What was he going on about? But before she could ask, this lovely old codger spun round and bustled after the Doctor up the steps, wagging a finger. 'Wait, wait! You'll get it all wrong without me.'

Which left Bill standing there, shut out, unsure of anything except … she really was Bill Potts. She just had to find some way to convince the Doctor of that.

6

The Glass Woman

In the TARDIS, Archie had been watching the monitor, trying to follow what was going on outside. He had no idea of the emotional background to what had just happened, but he'd seen enough sacrifice to know that these two splendid chaps—who seemed to be the same chap in some odd fashion—were walking into danger on his behalf.

He surely should go out there and stand with them. Or at least go to help that poor girl who seemed so hurt by the Doctor's rejection. And yet, if he was the ball that everyone involved here wanted to kick into the back of the net, it would be foolish to throw himself back onto the field. Wouldn't it?

The First Doctor wheezed and groaned to the top of the stairs, to find the Doctor had halted there, looking at an empty chair and the wall behind it. The wall was a bank of instruments, a computer made of diamonds, sleek and gleaming and powerful. The chair seemed to be of a piece with it, a latticework of circuitry. The First Doctor fitted his monocle to his reading eye and took a closer look at the wall. What he was looking at was also worrying, something similar to Rassilon's time scoop, but rather more subtle. 'Time-travel technology, obviously.'

'From the far future,' said the Doctor.

'I *know*.' The First Doctor turned to look at his foppish replacement and lost his monocle in astonishment. The man was wearing sunglasses. In the daytime. In a temporal anomaly. 'Sunglasses?'

'Sonic!'

'Indoors?'

'Yeah, but look at them, they're *sonic*.'

'That settles it,' snapped the First Doctor. 'I am not regenerating. No. You are cancelled.' Before he could add anything further, a beam of light cascaded into the chair, or perhaps throne would be a better description, because now sitting on it was a regal figure made entirely of glass. A delicate tracery of wires and circuitry ran across every surface of her transparent form. The wires trailed back to the wall behind her.

'What are you?' asked the Doctor.

The First Doctor had half expected him to come out with some ghastly so-called witticism about 'seeing right through her', but from the look on his fellow Doctor's face, humour was not on the menu tonight. The First Doctor wasn't much for jokes. He recalled once when his friend Steven had attempted to explain to him a message contained within a 'Christmas cracker'. The whole business had taken the best part of an hour and the First Doctor hadn't been left much the wiser at the end of it.

The woman waved a glass hand. Suddenly, the whole chamber was illuminated, with the same piercing light that was the sign of her presence. 'We are what awaits at the end of every life,' she said. Those alcoves, that also lined the walls here, began to illuminate, one by one. 'As every living soul dies, so we will appear.' In each alcove, the First Doctor could see another Glass Woman, shining with inner light. 'We take from you what we need, and return you to the moment of your death. We are Testimony.'

'Please stop,' the Doctor said, 'I'm worried you might actually start singing. So, you come from the distant future. You travel back in time, find people on the exact point of death, and what, harvest something from them?'

'Yes.' She looked between them. 'You are the same man, twice.' The First Doctor almost wanted to protest, but she was nevertheless literally correct. He was finding this talk of finding people at the moment of death especially worrying, given their own situation.

'You *steal* from the nearly dead,' said the Doctor. 'Why?'

'The same, yet so very different.'

'On behalf of the dying, what do we have that the future needs so badly?'

The First Doctor felt that this barely scratched the surface of the problem. 'And what does any of this have to do with a World War One Captain turning up at the South Pole, in the wrong decade, hmm?'

'We were returning him,' said the Glass Woman, 'to the appointed time and place of his death. An error in the timelines allowed him to escape into the wrong time zone.'

Inside the TARDIS, Archie had been watching the entire conversation. The picture on this telegraph thing had magically followed the Doctor up the stairs. Now he found himself having to hold on to the console of this ship of some kind to stop himself from toppling to the ground. So. So, that was what was happening here. This was … a grand cosmic authority of some kind. It knew when his time was up. When everyone's time was up, probably. There had been the sound of a shell overhead, hadn't there?

'Now his death must proceed as history demands,' said that calm, professional, voice.

Archie allowed himself to close his eyes, just for a moment.

The First Doctor understood the Glass Woman's point of view. History, after all, could not be changed, not one line. Except on the tiny number of occasions when, apparently, it could. Perhaps his future self had slightly more experience of these matters, had a more subtle sense of the fragile weave of space-time?

'Says who?' snarled the Doctor, which answered that question. 'Why? What's the purpose of any of this?'

'Are we to trust the Doctor of War, who walks in blood?' asked the Glass Woman, worryingly.

'Asked the time-travelling thief from the future,' finished the Doctor.

'We must negotiate.'

'So you can deliver a man to his death?'

'Yes.'

The First Doctor felt that if there was to be a negotiation then he should have a bigger part to play. 'If I may … who *were* you?' He leaned closer, inspecting her with his monocle, and was sure now, that he had it right, that he had got to the heart of this mystery. 'Who did you used to be, before you became … this? Hmm?'

The Doctor had whipped out his 'sonic screwdriver' and started examining her with it. 'She didn't "used to be" anyone, she's a computer-generated interface, connected to a multiform, inter-phasing databank.'

The First Doctor sighed at how much he had lost. 'Oh for heaven's sake, will you put that ridiculous buzzing toy away and *look* at the woman!' To his vague surprise, the Doctor did so, and the First Doctor pointed out—rude as it was to waggle his fingers in the face of a lady—his discovery. 'You see? Her face!

It's very slightly asymmetrical. If it were computer-generated, it would never produce that effect, hmm?'

The Doctor made a sound in the back of his throat, and adjusted his sonic sunglasses. 'Yes. You're absolutely right. I should have noticed that.'

'Well, it might help if you could see properly.' The First Doctor reached out, took the dratted things, and tossed them aside.

Of course, the fop went scrambling after them. Which was when a call came from the base of the steps, far below. 'Er, excuse me. Doctor?'

Oh dear.

The First Doctor and his replacement stepped as one to the top of the stairs, and looked down to see that that dratted Captain had stepped out of the TARDIS. The charming young lady was looking at him in surprise.

'Get back inside!' called the Doctor. 'Now!'

Archie dearly wished he was cowardly enough to obey. It turned out he wasn't. 'I was watching on the, well, whatever that thing is—'

'Mate ...' The young lady known as Bill was gesturing urgently to him to get back into the box.

'Remain inside the perimeter of the force field,' called the First Doctor.

It was going to take a moment to make them understand that he hadn't come out here out of foolishness. '—that window thing. Quite magical. I *could* hear what you were saying.'

'Get back in the TARDIS!' bellowed the Doctor.

Archie stopped, his toe an inch from the line the First Doctor had made. Here was the last point of safety. He understood that completely. He nodded to Bill. 'Miss. I don't think we've met.'

'Bill Potts. And nah, probably not.'

'Archie,' he said. 'Call me Archie.' Which got a pleasing grin. He turned to call up to the others. He had seen and heard the Doctors debating with some great authority that did not want, it had turned out, to *take* his life, but who insisted that his life was officially and formally over. The Queen, of Heaven, he presumed, though she hardly resembled she who was traditionally said to serve in that office, had produced Bill, and surely that meant there was an offer on the table, that she could be ... returned to life? In which case, his duty was utterly clear. 'I'm not quite sure, but it seemed to me that this young lady's life was being offered in exchange for my own. Now, as it happens, I think my number was pretty much up anyway—'

'What are you talking about?' Bill looked suddenly worried. Of course she did. 'Doctor, what's he talking about?'

'—so, might as well make it count for something, eh?'

He stepped over the line.

7

Escape to Danger

The Doctor stared in horror at what this fool of a man was doing. Now, Archie was looking again to Bill. 'I should be happy to take your place, if that will resolve this situation.'

'Accepted,' said the Glass Woman on the throne.

Bill shook her head. 'That is not happening. That is totally not happening.' She walked to the bottom of the stairs and looked up at the Doctors. 'Agreed?'

The Doctor felt that look on her face. Not for the first time, his sonic screwdriver had told him one thing, but his gut was telling him another. It couldn't be her. It *couldn't* be. It was just too convenient, her showing up again like this. And yet. And *yet* ...

'Tell me what to do, then,' he called. 'Bill Potts would tell me what to do.'

'What you always do,' she said. That look on her face had such faith in it. 'Serve at the pleasure of the human race.'

He felt the ghost of a smile on his face. For the first time in days, he felt slight hope and gave it its due. He was dying, he had perhaps moments left, but they could be long moments, now he was outside time, useful moments. He spun on his heel and looked to the Glass Woman. 'Here's what's going to happen. First, I'm going to escape!' He felt the old man beside him stiffen in shock, and nodded to him. 'You, with me.'

And he actually turned his back on the creature who seemingly had authority and power over all time and space and started back down the stairs.

The old man scampered after him. 'Where are we going?'

'Escape is not possible,' called the Glass Woman, not quite so calmly now.

'It is possible, and it's happening, and I'm taking Bill and the Captain with me.'

'Why are your advertising your intentions?' the old boy whispered. 'Can't you stop boasting, even for a moment?'

By now they were both at the bottom of the stairs. The Doctor indicated his older self to the Glass Woman. 'I'm taking Mr Pastry too. I could do with a laugh.'

The First Doctor was looking blankly at him. He was obviously yet to meet the actor who played that character. What was his name? Oh yeah, Richard

Hearne. The Doctor's second incarnation had once helped the old man escape from a balloon factory in Epping.

The Glass Woman had stood up from her throne. She was louder this time, actually becoming angry. 'Escape is not possible!'

'Oh,' the Doctor called up to her, 'I'm going to do way more than escape. I'm going to find out who you are and what you're doing, and if I don't like it, I will come back. And I will stop you. I will stop all of you.'

The First Doctor was staring at him like he was a rebellious teenager. 'Who the hell do you think you are?'

'I'm the Doctor.' He had said it so often, so often it had been all he had to cling to, just as it was now. But usually the voice it was meant to shout down was strictly *inner*.

'No, *I* am the Doctor,' his younger self fumed. 'Who you are, I cannot begin to imagine!' Because of course his former self would have gone about this completely differently, and would by now be sipping cocktails with the Glass Woman, and be wheedling his way into unbolting her plans, having accidentally got engaged to one of the other glass women, probably.

'Then let us show you, Doctor,' called the Glass Woman, who would probably have preferred the First Doctor's approach, given how calm and straightforward she was trying to make the business of theft and extortion. 'See who you will become!'

The chamber started to swirl with holographic images, around the Doctors, Bill and the Captain. Oh dear, was she really going to show the old man the full box set? It'd be kind of tough if she got him onside and, knowing the First Doctor, that wasn't outside the realm of possibility. 'No! No, don't do that!' He was surprised at how desperate his voice had sounded. Because … yeah, there was more to it than that, wasn't there, Doctor? The old man was looking at him having registered that tone. Then he looked back to the images.

There he was, in his previous lives, tricking Davros into using that terrible weapon to destroy his own race's home world. There he was, strutting along thinking of himself as the Time Lord Victorious, when Adelaide Brooke had put a gun to her own head and showed him the folly of his ways. There he was during the Time War, arranging for Daleks to be gunned down, arranging for the closing of the Advent of Woe, arranging for the Nightmare Child to never arise and forever be aware of its non-existence. There he was staggering through Cybermen, making them fall around him. There was Adric. There was Donna. There was Bill.

He made himself look to the First Doctor. The expression on his face as he gazed at the images was shocked, angry … scared of the future. Then he turned to look at the Doctor, accusing. Beside him, Bill was actually smiling at what she saw in the floating shapes. It was like she knew him … better. Forgave him. Understood. Had shared what they'd been through. But no, he couldn't allow himself the comfort of that thought.

'The Doctor has walked in blood through all of time and space,' the Glass Woman said. 'The Doctor has many names. He is the Shadow of the Valeyard, the butcher of Skull Moon, the Last Tree of Garsennon, the destroyer of Skaro. He is the Doctor of War.'

And it was all true, thought the Doctor. He had allowed himself to learn the truth about his supposed destruction of his own people, he had been absolved of that, and yet there was so much else. Was he a good man? That was the question he had asked himself. He had decided he was just a man. And yet … and yet … to be faced with an earlier self, the self that had first decided to be more than just a man, to be a hero, and one who somehow went about that with some dignity too … well, here was perspective. A bit too much bloody perspective.

The images suddenly flew back to their source. The display was over. 'What … what was that?' asked the First Doctor.

'To be fair,' said the Doctor, 'they cut out all the jokes.'

The First Doctor wasn't about to leave it at that, but no, this was playing into the hands of the Glass Woman, that debate was what she wanted. So no more.

The Doctor grabbed his sonic screwdriver. 'Do what I do when I do it.' He hit the button to activate the sequence he had programmed in while he was still in the TARDIS. He had hoped to use the ship to escape, but he had also been working on Plan B. The iris under the ship snapped open. The police box plummeted, the chains that were still attached to the clamps on its sides unreeling at high speed. 'Now!'

He led all four of them to sprint for those chains. They got it. They followed him. They leapt. They grabbed one chain each.

And then they were out, plunging into the freezing air, speeding towards the ground with the TARDIS dropping below them, above the beautiful sight of Antarctica in darkness. The Doctor could still see tiny lights down there. Just as well time had halted – and it still was, because the snow they were falling through was motionless – or there'd have been missiles flying at them by now. He couldn't help it, he burst out laughing at the sheer exhilaration. He had gotten away with it again! He could still say that, here at the end of his life! He looked upward to Bill, and she was grinning too. He shared the smile with her, just for a moment. But the doubt of her made him not quite able to hold it. He looked to the other two. They weren't looking so happy about it, but never mind, because here came the ground! They'd kept the Glass Woman so busy that she hadn't bothered moving her ship. They only had a couple of hundred feet to cover, albeit straight down. Still, what was a little gravity between friends?

'You are not escaping!' called the Glass Woman's voice from right next to his ear. Yeah, he thought, how's that going for you?

A moment later, however, he discovered exactly how well, as the chains slammed to a halt. They all had to grab hold to stop themselves being thrown clear. The TARDIS was left dangling, just about twenty feet above the frozen wastes. The four of them were considerably higher up than that.

'Come on!' he shouted, and started to scramble precipitously down the chain. A fall from this height ... oh come on, don't be ridiculous, Doctor. He was reconciled to that, no point in fearing it now. He saw the others were doing their best to follow, the First Doctor wide-eyed with the effort. What would happen if the old guy regenerated now, in a different way to how he remembered it? Would he even turn into the annoying bumbler with the big trousers? Or would they rip a hole in space-time and destroy the universe? Ironic ending, that one.

Bit of a shaggy dog story. He banished the bleak thoughts and leapt for the roof of the TARDIS, hit it, held on, and started climbing down. Horribly, the TARDIS started to rise once more, the chain now being hoisted back into the ship. 'Jump!' he shouted. 'Jump!'

He and the other three did so at the same moment, and all hit the ground together. He rolled over and winced, but no, no damage, he just had to take a moment to concentrate, to hold back the change ... and managed once again to do so. He looked around to find his three allies slowly getting to their feet. Above them, the TARDIS was rushing upwards, beyond their reach.

Bill looked to him. 'What do we do now?'

'Run!'

'Where? They've got the TARDIS.'

'Yes, that's exactly what they're supposed to think.'

Bill looked between him and where the police box was now being dragged back into the hull of the enormous spaceship. 'Yeah, but they do though.'

'They've got *my* TARDIS.' The Doctor pointed at his younger self. 'Over to you, Mary Berry.'

Of course, the reference was lost on his younger self, who was yet to meet the celebrity chef he so resembled. It had been his ... third incarnation, hadn't it, who'd spent that wonderful summer with her on that narrowboat in the Cotswolds?

The First Doctor suddenly cottoned on, and dusted snow off his waistcoat, his imperious stage magician self once again. 'They have, as you say, the TARDIS. So what's the last thing they're going to expect us to do, hmm?' He produced his TARDIS key with a flourish. 'Escape in the TARDIS!'

8

A Dance to the Music of Time Lords

'Come on!' The First Doctor headed off through the suspended snow, taking Archie's arm. 'This way, my good fellow.'

'I'm … a little confused,' said Archie.

'What, only a little?' chuckled the First Doctor. 'Dear me, dear me, I must be slipping!'

'What's going on with the snow?' Bill asked the Doctor, catching up.

He couldn't quite look at her. 'Time has stopped.'

To his annoyance, she grabbed his arm and turned him to face her. 'Okay, so you don't think I'm real yet, do you?'

'We've got to keep moving!'

But she held him back. She was so desperate for him to give in to this hope. 'Except you rescued me, so maybe you do a little. Listen, I don't know how I got here, but I am actually me—' She stopped, thankfully. She was looking past him. 'Doctor … is that another TARDIS?'

The Doctor saw that the First Doctor had reached his ship and was unlocking it. Archie, beside him, was nodding at the sight of it, as if one more impossibility didn't make much difference, really. 'No,' said the Doctor, 'it's another of the same TARDIS. Inside, quickly!'

'Hang on,' she just had time to say, as he seized her hand and pulled her through the door after the other two, 'the windows are the wrong—'

She stopped when she was hauled into the console room, and the Doctor had slammed the door behind them, and she got to do the 'amazed at what's inside the box' moment a second time. Because this interior wasn't his own stylish modern installation, but the plain white look of factory settings, offset with the plinths on which his predecessor displayed his precious things, the overall effect being like the classical and modernist wings of an art gallery that had been involved in a terrible accident.

'Take off,' the Doctor shouted. 'Now! Deep space, anywhere!'

The First Doctor was already doing his routine little dance around the console, with the power building up as he did it, because, of course, he hadn't worked out how to boil it down to a bunch of code routines and one big lever yet. The Doctor resisted the urge to march over there and … probably short circuit everything, actually. Best leave the old boy to it. The First Doctor raised a finger to make him wait, then triumphantly hit a control. The engines roared, the central column started to rise and fall, the room lurched, and they all had to grab hold of the console or fall over. At least, the Doctor reflected, the old lad had managed to avoid rendering his passengers unconscious. Must be one of his good days.

'We are in the Vortex,' the old man declared.

'Tell you what,' noted the Captain, delighted at having an idea he could put his finger on, 'these police boxes, they're ever so good, aren't they?'

'The navigation systems don't function properly,' the First Doctor said. 'I'm unable to program our flight with any accuracy.'

'Yeah,' sighed the Doctor, 'I remember.' He wandered over and had a quick fiddle with the controls, just enough to sort things for this one journey. Just enough to let the old girl understand what he was planning.

His previous self looked up at him, appraising, and also ... disapproving.

'What you saw,' said the Doctor, 'your future. I suppose it can't be easy, seeing all your regrets in advance.' Though, thankfully, if these things worked out as they usually did, when the Time Lords didn't arrange things so that only certain edits were made, both of them would walk away from this with only the vaguest memory of what they'd experienced.

The First Doctor looked back to his instruments, not being able as yet to formulate a reply.

'Those things have to happen,' the Doctor went on. 'All of them. The future depends on it.'

'You misremembered,' the First Doctor said.

'I'm sorry?'

'Borusa's lesson. "In hope you are at your weakest … in strength you are at your worst."' He looked up at him. 'It wasn't weakness he was warning us about.'

That … rather stopped the Doctor in his tracks. He actually *had* forgotten that. He had forgotten the important bit, over and over, as if forgetting it had become the most reliable part of his character. Yet his first self never had. 'Yeah, well,' he muttered, 'Borusa and his terrible poems, look how he ended up.' Because his old tutor had hardly practised what he preached, had been definitively hoisted on his own petard. Which, of course, indicated the truth of what he'd said.

'He had a point, on that occasion,' said the First Doctor. And, as if he could see he'd made his own point, he offered the Doctor a slight smile. 'Although his poems were truly awful.'

'Doctor,' Bill stepped forward to interrupt. 'Where are we?'

'What does it look like? Bill Potts could figure it out.'

She looked aghast at him, once again. He wondered why he kept doubting her. Perhaps he'd been kicked too many times, been fooled too many times. But before she could reply, the First Doctor had come bustling forward. 'Oh, my dear, I'm so sorry, I appear to be forgetting my manners. This is the ship. *My* ship. I built her.'

The Doctor coughed, loudly and significantly. What a whopper!

The First Doctor ignored him. 'She is known as TARDIS. The initials stand for—'

'Time And Relative Dimension In Space.' Bill said it with him. And she hadn't even gone for the plural on the D word, like he sometimes did when he decided to flirt with the translation circuits. She'd actually noticed which version he regarded as traditional, the Doctor realised, and used it for this old man who she must now be thinking was this ship's original owner. That quickness of thought was so like her. Wasn't it? She saw him looking. He managed not to turn away.

'How do you ...?' The First Doctor frowned and nodded. 'Oh, I see, you travel with him!'

'Used to.' She looked wistful for a second. 'Kind of miss it.' The look on her face broke the Doctor's hearts all over again.

'Well, my dear,' said the First Doctor, patting her shoulder, 'he clearly misses you. That ship of his is in dire need of a good spring clean!'

Before Bill could entirely grasp his unfortunate meaning, the Doctor hustled his former self back to the console. 'No no no, stop, stop. Stop talking, look at the astral map, concentrate on that. Oh, look at all the lovely blinking lights—'

The First Doctor jerked from his grasp, affronted, but they were interrupted by Bill. 'He's you,' she said. They both looked at her in surprise. 'He's you. Well, you're both ... you're both each other.' Archie had raised a finger, about to ask a question, but instead he opted to just lower it again. 'You told me you had different faces. I never quite got what that meant, but if it's true, I think he's one of your old ones, yeah?'

'Oh,' said the Doctor, smiling at how good she was (or rather, he had to remind himself, how good an impersonation), 'he's a *very* old one.'

'The original, in fact!' noted the First Doctor.

'You know,' said Archie, 'I find I'm lagging behind a tiny bit again ...'

The Doctor clapped his hands together. 'Right! Any questions?'

'Yeah,' said Bill, 'why didn't you keep the hair?'

'The hair?'

Bill pointed. 'The hair's awesome.'

The Doctor stared in horror as the First Doctor flirtatiously flicked back what remained of his locks and chuckled. Of all the ... What about *his* ... ? He had put a lot of work into—! 'Terrible question!' he said. 'Boring question! Here's a better one.' He took the sonic sunglasses from his pocket and slid them back onto his nose.

'Not those again!' called the First Doctor. 'I forbid it!'

You should have found the dimmer switch, then, thought the Doctor, but he didn't honour Mr Because I'm Worth It with a reply. He tapped a control on the side of the sunglasses, and a picture appeared on the monitor, high up on the wall, where everyone had to risk repetitive strain injury to see it. It was the Glass Woman, an image that the sunglasses had automatically recorded earlier. 'There you are,' he said, 'I was right. Asymmetrical.'

'*I* said that!' gasped the First Doctor.

'Same difference.' Very much enjoying this, he went to his earlier self, took off the sunglasses, and shoved them onto his face. The First Doctor reacted like a cat who'd been thrown into a coal cellar. 'If her face *was* based on a human original, perhaps identifying who that was will tell us what we need to know about Testimony.'

'Why,' demanded the old man, 'am I wearing these?'

'Because I love it,' said the Doctor, 'never take those off.'

The First Doctor suddenly stopped, his hand reaching for the controls on the frame. 'What's "browser history"?'

The Doctor suddenly recalled one of River's little habits concerning their personal communications and … cat pictures, yes, that was it, cat pictures. He grabbed the sunglasses off his other self's face and dropped them back into his own pocket in one smooth motion. He saw Bill grinning at him and ignored her. He was already busy at the controls. 'I'm trying to find a match for that face in the TARDIS databank, but there's hardly anything in it yet.'

'My dear fellow,' said the First Doctor, 'one face in all of history, in all of space and time …'

'Yeah, we need a bigger database.'

'I doubt even the Matrix on Gallifrey could quite run to that.'

The Doctor had had a terrible thought. 'No. No. We'd need something better than the Matrix … ' He wandered away to think.

'So …' said Archie, trying to keep on top of things, 'we're trying to track the glass lady, yes?'

'Basically,' said Bill. 'I think.'

'I've said it before, and I'll say it again,' said Archie. 'Our policemen are wonderful!'

The Glass Woman was watching those who were trying to escape her. She was watching through the eyes she had access to, inside the TARDIS. She was watching Archie, and she was watching the two different versions of the same person, one of whom actually seemed, to judge by the look on his face, to have had an idea about what they might do to get away.

The Glass Woman was very good with faces. She had seen so many.

These poor people had no idea what she was or what she stood for. They still thought they could get away.

9

The Ruins

'What a striking-looking creature,' said Archie. He was looking at the image of the Glass Woman. 'Quite beautiful really, isn't she?'

'If you like ladies made of glass.' Bill was looking at the image too. There was something about the Glass Woman that was way too familiar for her liking, something about her that was buried in the memories she couldn't access. She shivered.

'Well,' said the First Doctor, 'aren't *all* ladies made of glass, in a way?'

Archie actually chortled at that. 'Oh, very good, sir, very good.'

'Are we, now?' Bill looked over to her Doctor, to see him wincing like he'd just stood on a piece of Lego. He looked as if he desperately wanted her to let that go. So she didn't.

The First Doctor clasped his lapels. 'Oh, my dear! I hope it does not offend you to know that I *do* have some experience of the fairer sex.'

'Me too,' she said simply.

'Good Lord,' said Archie.

'Loads,' she mouthed to him, with a smile.

There was a sudden lurch, and they all stumbled. The Doctor looked up from the controls as the central column slowed to a halt. Bill got the feeling he'd done that deliberately. He hit another control, and the doors whirred open. Bill went to see what awaited them. The Doctor joined her. Under a hellish red sky stood the stark, blackened ruins of what looked to be a science fiction city that had lived through seven seasons of *Game of Thrones*. Giant statues had been broken in half, domes had cracked open, and spires leaned precipitously against adjoining buildings. An alien breeze brought the smell of ... burning. Of rotting meat. Of death. The remains of moons tumbled overhead, impossibly close, as if even gravity were failing, and nearby a larger planetoid was ripping itself apart. 'Where are we?'

The First Doctor was still examining the readouts on the console. 'You steered the ship! You piloted her perfectly! We are billions of years in your future. And, apparently, at the very centre of the universe!'

'Out there,' said the Doctor, indicating the wasteland beyond, 'is the most comprehensive database ever assembled of *all* life, everywhere. There *is* one little problem.'

'Which is?' said Bill.

The Doctor grinned his scary grin. 'It wants to kill me.' With that, he strode out onto this new world. Bill followed. She was quite surprised that, after all he had seen, and considering the condition he was in, Archie got to the doors before the First Doctor did.

They walked together, a few steps along the dark canyon of a street on which the TARDIS had landed. The shadows on every side felt like death looking down on them. Rustling vines draped the shattered walls. Roots writhed up through the cracked concrete at their feet. There was a sense of rustling, restless movement everywhere, like the planet was full of rats, squirming a centimetre below the surface. They stopped to gaze at the jagged, ruined skyline.

Archie, in particular, seemed almost physically hurt by what he was seeing. She guessed, from what the Doctor had said about the situation the Captain had come from, that here was just more of the same, another world of the same, when immediately before this he'd been seeing wonders that had let him escape. She couldn't help but feel for him. Product of his time or not, here was someone who'd also been willing to offer his life so she could live hers. She didn't believe he'd do anything other than still honour that bargain. 'What,' he whispered, 'in the name of sanity, *is* this place?'

'The Weapon Forges of Villengard,' said the Doctor. 'Once the nightmare of the seven galaxies. Now home to the dispossessed.'

'What happened?' asked the First Doctor.

'You,' said the Doctor.

The First Doctor caught his meaning and looked sharply at him. He really didn't want to own the future he was being promised. 'I don't understand,' he snapped. 'How were you able to pilot the ship here?'

The Doctor sighed. 'Because she's not a ship, she's the TARDIS. Because you didn't build her, you stole her. Because you didn't steal her, she stole you. Because she'll never take you where you want to go, but she'll always put you where you need to be. Which, right now, is here.'

The old man waved all that aside with an angry gesture, but it was clear from his face that he'd taken it in.

'Because of a database?' asked Bill.

'The biggest database in this galaxy, this sector, possibly anywhere.'

Bill realised that Archie had suddenly become alert, was drawing his revolver. 'I say,' he said, 'I think there's something moving over there.' He kept one eye on the shadows at the side of the street as he spun through the chambers. 'I only have five rounds.'

He was right too, there was something moving in the gutters there, really pretty close.

'Be careful, Captain,' advised the First Doctor. 'Step away, please.'

'Probably just rats,' said Archie. 'I'm used to rats.'

Suddenly, something launched itself at Archie's face.

It was a blob of tentacles, a pulsating, hissing mass of fury. It latched itself onto his head and he fell, his revolver going flying, his screams muffled by this obscene thing. He crashed to the ground and started to try to claw it from his face.

Bill and the Doctors ran to his aid. Bill got her fingers into the flesh of the creature, tried to physically haul it from him, but the contact stung her skin and she had to pull her fingers back, crying out. The First Doctor started to helplessly thump at it with his hand inside his cloak.

But the Doctor had leapt back, had pulled out his screwdriver and was hitting controls frantically. 'It's okay!' he shouted. 'It's okay, I've got it!'

The sonic screwdriver suddenly shrieked with a higher note. The creature squealed. Bill realised she could see a mouth in it, a horrible, quivering orifice with … metal teeth?

And then it was gone, releasing Archie and away into the shadows again.

Bill went quickly to Archie. He was lying there, panting, his face scratched. It hadn't had time to do him much damage, thank God. He started to cough and splutter. He looked as if he wanted to sob, but didn't know how, all the pain of war back on his face in a moment. Then he took a deep breath and calmed himself and looked at her and nodded, as if acknowledging her absolutely, as if, by coming to his aid, she was entirely his comrade now. Bill felt that. She gently pushed her fist into his shoulder, acknowledging him back.

The Doctor helped him to his feet. 'Deep breaths. Deep breaths. Just breathe, Captain, you'll be fine.'

'That creature,' said the First Doctor, 'it looked … familiar.'

'It's mutated a bit,' said the Doctor, ominously, 'but yes, I should think it did.'

Bill had been looking to see where the thing had gone. She could still see movement in that dark gutter. Lots of movement. And now there was movement from beyond the gutter, from up past the sides of the street … both sides … there were now things squirming in the shadows everywhere she looked.

The whole city was suddenly swarming with the creatures, alive with them. The air was filled with the sounds of their squealing and gibbering. It was all focused on the Doctor's party.

They were surrounded.

10

Heart of Glass

'What are those things?' asked Bill.

The Doctor had hoped that they wouldn't attract this much attention, but like that was ever going to happen. 'What we came here for,' he said. 'The biggest database in the galaxy.' Bill stared at him. To her it must be as if Wikipedia had suddenly grown tentacles. 'They'll settle down in a moment.'

They did. With no new targets venturing close to the darkness they loved, the creatures gradually skittered away. They were pack animals at heart, after all. No individual courage was to be found in them. The Doctor turned to check on Archie, who was being tended to by the First Doctor. 'Come along, my dear chap, you'll be fine.'

'Get him back into the TARDIS,' said the Doctor. There was no reason this man had to be forced to confront more monsters.

'Oh, did someone put you in charge of this little expedition, hmm?' said the old man. However, he did as he was told, helping the only slightly protesting soldier back towards safety.

Bill had gone to watch the creatures skittering around, running for cover, upwards, sideways, into the cracks, wherever they usually hid in the ruins. The Doctor surveyed them too. They had evolved so far from their usual commanding selves, and were, at the same time, just like them.

'So, do we talk to them?' said Bill. 'Ask them questions? How does it work?'

'*We* don't do anything,' said the Doctor, grabbing her arm and hauling her back towards the TARDIS, hoping to get her there before she started yelling too much. 'I do.'

'Oh no, no, no!'

'You're going to wait in the TARDIS.'

'Why?'

He'd led her to the doors of the TARDIS. He found he could still hardly look at her. She was like his conscience made flesh, mostly in that her existence was unreliable. 'I need you to look after the Captain.'

'You're lying. You think I'm a duplicate, a trick.'

'I don't know what I think.'

'You don't trust me. You don't think I'm really me. Tell me the truth!'

In this incarnation, the Doctor could never have resisted that invitation to honest bluntness. 'I don't trust you, and I don't think you're really you.' He saw the effect his words had on her; he'd known what they would do. 'But if there is the slightest chance that Bill Potts is alive and standing in front of me, I will not, under any circumstances, endanger her life again.'

'Seriously. You're looking right at me. And you don't even know I'm here.'

'Correct. I ask you to respect that, and to respect *me*—'

'You're an arse, you know that? You're a stupid bloody arse.'

'—as I have always respected ... *you*.'

There was an anguished silence between them.

The door of the TARDIS burst open, and the First Doctor stuck his head out, wagging a finger at Bill. 'If I hear any more language like that from you, young lady, you're in for a jolly good smacked bottom!' He slammed the door behind him and vanished back inside.

The Doctor and Bill continued to look at each other. The anguished silence had now changed a bit in nature. Bill suddenly burst out laughing; he almost joined in, but the wincing rather got in the way. 'Well! Doctor!'

'Can we please ... *please* ...?'

'I mean, I'm a broad-minded girl and everything ...'

'Can we just pretend that never—?'

'I realise we have this professor-student thing going on ...'

'Can we never, ever, talk about this again?'

She was suddenly serious again. 'Yeah, I hope we talk about it loads. I hope we spend years laughing about it.'

His hearts could have broken. 'Me too.'

She saw the look on his face and seemed to decide it was enough for her. She nodded, and opened the door of the TARDIS. 'Come back alive.'

'Be here when I do.'

She went inside.

He felt suddenly weak. He had to lean on the old police box to keep upright. The strain of remaining himself. In all his years of life in this incarnation, he had finally learned some lessons about human life that his other selves had not. He had enjoyed, for decades, the dream of a normal existence. He had had love, long-lived love. He still wore his wedding ring. This time, if he allowed the regeneration to happen, he wouldn't just be sacrificing some iconic hero, he would be *losing a life*. He would be losing it *anyway*. So why not … why not simply …

Yes, he had made up his mind, he had made up his mind before he had even set off on this diversion. He opened his palm and saw it, the phoenix fire that wanted to consume him. He concentrated, and closed his hand … and the flame was banished again. For a moment.

He had just a few more things to learn yet.

Inside the TARDIS, the First Doctor had found the brandy, behind one of the console room roundels. The last time he had raided this drinks cabinet had been that time one Christmas with dear Steven and Sara Kingston … Kingsley … ah, yes, Kingdom. 'Perhaps another nip of brandy?' he suggested to Archie, who was recovering from his ordeal in a rather nice chair the First Doctor had found in Pimlico in 1927. He was anxious to do his part to help the Captain, and then be off to join his other self once more. He was anxious about haste in all things at the moment, because he could feel the change pounding at him, insisting. Still, he would hold it off. He had no intention of giving in to the sheer impertinence of his biology. He was resolved, yes, he was, to stand up to it, *whatever* happened. He poured out a glass, resisted drinking it himself, and noted that he had already made that mark on the side of the bottle, and had just dropped the level of liquid beneath it. He had possibly been a bit worried about the youngsters in his crew finding this supply. 'Oh. *This* is where it went!'

Bill had gone to Archie, and was looking at the scratches on his face, presumably attempting to ascertain whether or not they might be infected. 'I'll look after him.'

'Good girl. Quite right.' He set the bottle and glass down on the console beside them, and felt it necessary to deploy his wagging finger once again. If there was one thing he would not stand for, it was intemperate language. 'Now, young lady, I don't want to have to repeat myself—'

'I don't think any of us want that.'

Excellent. He nodded at her appropriate agreement with his scolding. 'I'll see you both presently.' He activated the door control, and headed out to join the fop and make sure he didn't trip over his own feet.

The Glass Woman watched as her target, this Captain, put his hands to his face. He had already caused himself undue suffering, when all he had to do was surrender to her. He had tried, but these copies of the same person were preventing him from coming to her. She heard him being offered brandy. 'Please,' he said.

A hand came into view, reaching for the bottle.

The Glass Woman was displeased to see that she had nearly given herself away. The hand was made of glass.

11

Old Friends

The Doctor hadn't exactly been overjoyed to see that the First Doctor did indeed intend to return and accompany him on his mission. They made their way together through the overgrown streets, aware this time of the thin, high voices of the beings that gibbered and scuttled in the shadows.

'These creatures,' said the First Doctor, 'what are they?'

Had he really not got it yet? 'Old friends of ours,' said the Doctor, 'but they've really come out of their shell.' Ahead, he finally saw on the horizon what his rough mental map of this place had told him was out there. He pointed. 'That tower over there, the only one with its top still on. That's where my friend is.'

The First Doctor squinted into the distance. Atop the tower, a faint light could be seen, the only light on this world. Someone was home. '"Out of their shell", you said; do you mean …?'

Suddenly, pain spasmed through the Doctor's head, agony from his body. He cried out, had to stagger to a chunk of wall and grab hold of it to stay on his feet.

'Are you all right?' asked the First Doctor urgently.

'I'll be … fine in a moment.'

'What's the matter?'

What, did he think they were both in exactly the same predicament, that he'd just worn himself thin through centuries of holding on? He had wounds, great burns and lesions from combat. His mind was holding back this pain as well as the fires of regeneration. 'I *died* a few hours ago. Then I refused to regenerate. It catches up with you.' He flapped a hand to wave away the retreating pain. 'Like a big lunch.'

'I did exactly the same,' insisted the First Doctor.

With a groan, the Doctor found a convenient place to sit on the chunk of wall. They were far enough from the shadows here. He indicated for the old man to sit by him. He wasn't going to be going anywhere for a while, after all. 'I know you did, but why? I don't remember this.' Because of the temporal amnesia caused by their meeting, or something more sinister? It wasn't to do with what the old man had seen of his future, was it? 'Why are you refusing the regeneration?'

The First Doctor sat. 'Why are you?'

'I asked first.'

'In point of fact, I'm earlier in our timeline, so …' The First Doctor twinkled, and tapped him on the leg.

'*I* asked first!' The Doctor couldn't help but join in his chuckle. But as the First Doctor's laughter faded, the humour on his face faded with it. The Doctor felt that he was looking into the eyes of a very old man. The old man was looking ashamed. 'Fear,' he whispered. 'I'm afraid. Very, very afraid. I … do not normally admit that to anyone else.'

The Doctor took pity on him. 'Don't worry, technically you still haven't.' It took a moment for the First Doctor to understand, then he looked irked at the lack of seriousness in the face of his admission. The Doctor put a hand on his shoulder to stop him from standing in anger. 'It'll be fine. You just have to let go. Just let yourself go. Hold tight to everything you believe. Jump into the darkness. And hope you land safely.' He remembered how it had always been. If only he could say these same words to himself and believe them. 'Afterwards, don't go swimming for half an hour.'

'I don't know if I can.'

'Look at the stars.' The Doctor nodded upwards.

The First Doctor looked up, beyond the thin red atmosphere, at the sweep of distant galaxies arranged equidistantly from this supposed central point of the universe. Here was a Milky Way of Milky Ways, a long way from everywhere. 'What about them?'

'Half of them will go out,' said the Doctor, 'if you don't carry on and do the things you're supposed to do.'

The First Doctor looked back to him, hawk-like. 'How many more will go dark if *you* don't?' The Doctor found he couldn't reply. 'You have done this before. Many times, I assume. What is stopping you now, hmm?'

'The … changes have been getting bigger,' muttered the Doctor. 'Stronger, more volcanic. Last time I wiped out a whole Dalek fleet.'

The First Doctor made a disapproving noise. 'You're afraid too.'

'I suppose I should admit that to myself.'

'I think you just did.'

The Doctor felt he could try to explain some of it to the youngster, try to make him see why he himself was right to feel afraid, why the First Doctor was wrong to. The old man was done, the Doctor knew him as something finished and put upon a shelf, whereas he was whole and here and had achieved what none of the others had: he'd had the entirety of a real, human life. 'Who I am right now, my consciousness, my conscience, my … soul … is about to rip apart. Someone else will walk back out of the storm. A stranger.' He looked into those old young eyes again. They shared for a moment that feeling of being haunted by their own future. 'And that stranger will be me.'

The First Doctor paused, then decided to venture on with his reply. 'My problem is slightly different. I was just about reconciled to giving in and letting go, as you say.'

'Yes.'

'And then I met you. The stranger from the storm is standing in front of me. And I don't think I like myself.'

Ah. So it *was* that. 'Oh,' sighed the Doctor, remembering some of the previous occasions when they'd had this family reunion, 'you never will.'

Suddenly, they were bathed in a beam of white light. The Doctor shielded his eyes and saw that the beam was coming from their destination, from the very top of the tower.

'That'll be my friend,' he said. 'I think he knows I'm here.' He stood up and stepped away from the First Doctor, so he was silhouetted at the centre of the beam, and began to wave his arms. 'Hello! Here I am! How are you? How's things?'

An energy bolt blasted away the ground at his feet. The Doctor leapt out of the way, but then came another, and another. He found himself violently throwing himself from one side to the other, dancing to avoid death. The First Doctor reached out a hand, grabbed him, and hauled him back into cover behind the ruined wall.

'I was right,' said the Doctor, casually. 'He knows I'm here.'

'Why do you keep calling him your friend?'

'He's got a great big gun, are you suggesting I insult him?' He stood up again and stepped back into the light. 'Excuse me!' This time the ground nearby erupted upwards in an explosion. There was another, and another, close enough to send the Doctor staggering. 'Landmines,' he explained to the First Doctor. 'He's setting them off. This whole place is booby trapped.' He pulled out his sonic screwdriver and fiddled with the settings.

'Can you detect them?'

'No, but I can blow them all up.' He sent a wide-beam sonic pulse at exactly the right frequency all the way down the path between him and the tower, and was rewarded with a very satisfying series of detonations. The First Doctor skipped about about at every fireball that burst into the sky. Finally, the smoke and flame died down. 'There you go, all done.'

'There could have been one right underneath us!'

'Yeah, but it's not the kind of mistake you have to live with.' That was the other thing about his centuries of additional experience, he was a little more willing to roll the dice. Or perhaps it was just at this point he didn't give a damn. What the hell, his clothes were already ruined, might as well mess up the bodywork too. It wasn't like he was planning to trade the old thing in.

But now there came a hissing and shuffling from all around them. Great clouds of dust had been thrown up by the explosions, and through the murk the Doctor could see the creatures moving, massing, advancing, disturbed by the concussions, as his friend in the tower must have been aware they would be.

They came at them at high speed, rushing through the dust, flailing and gibbering, dozens of them. They launched themselves straight at the Doctor and down he went, down into a mass of the tearing, biting, sucking things, tentacles wrapping around his neck, trying to press against his eyes, trying to invade his mouth. He hadn't taken enough of a breath to cry out. He forced a hand into his pocket, fumbling for the sonic, but realised with horror that he'd dropped it as they'd grabbed him.

12

The Tower

Suddenly the creatures starting squirming away from the Doctor. Impacts had come raining down through their bodies so hard that the Doctor could feel them; he realised that his younger self was actually thumping the things.

'Unhand him!' the First Doctor was shouting, his voice muffled by the sheer number of alien bodies. 'That man is unarmed! Leave him alone!' Which was all well and good, and it had given him a moment's respite, but surely the old man must realise that the only way to get him out of here would be—

The familiar sound of the sonic screwdriver was music to the Doctor's ears. The wrong music, for just a second, which made him bellow, but then the old lad got it and the creatures started jumping off him, racing to get away, scrambling to be first to throw themselves off of him … and swiftly he was lying there, clear above him, managing a breath and seeing the First Doctor standing there, proudly and awkwardly, holding the sonic screwdriver as if it was a fragile ornament.

'Are you all right?' the old man asked.

The Doctor managed a smile. 'That was it.'

'What was what?'

The Doctor pointed at the screwdriver. 'My very first time.' Suddenly, the light from the tower washed across them again, the dust having settled enough to allow it through. The Doctor struggled to his feet, retrieved the screwdriver, and called up into the light again. 'Okay, calm down, hold your horses—'

He had to dodge another couple of energy bolts, but they were becoming almost formal in nature, more of a greeting than anything else … even if they were pitched in the medium of excited plasma.

'No, just scan me. Go on, scan me. Because I've got big news for you. I'm dying!'

The energy bolts stopped. A buzzing came from the tower. Then the nature of the searchlight changed. It became a scanner beam, lines of information twisting around the Doctor's body and being immediately relayed back to the being in the tower.

'You see? It's true. Dying.'

The light snapped off.

'Now, be honest with yourself. Wouldn't you like to see that up close?'

There was a moment of silence, then a grinding noise. The Doctor looked to the tower in the distance.

In its base a door was opening. The Doctor tried to step forward, but again came the agonies he was holding back, fighting to change him, here and now. But then the First Doctor was beside him, propping him up, and he managed to hold them back, yet stay alive, once again, for a little while. 'Will you help me over there?' he whispered.

'Why are you doing this?' asked the old man. 'What's this *for*?' Because he'd surely realised this was a bit of a hoo-hah just to consult a library. This had to be the library of all libraries, and his motivation for it must therefore go way beyond an inquiry to help a random innocent like the Captain.

'Bill,' said the Doctor. The First Doctor considered, nodded, and then bore his weight towards the tower. 'Come on,' the Doctor couldn't resist adding. 'Up and at 'em, Corporal Jones.' As ever, the reference was lost on his younger self, who knew nothing of Clive Dunn's bumbling *Dad's Army* hero. Only should he reach his sixth incarnation would he find himself touring the London pubs with the sitcom star—and there was still every chance he'd refuse even to reach his second.

Archie was more holding the brandy than drinking it. The glass was shaking in his hand. He didn't trust his surroundings enough to allow himself as much as he wanted. Also, he didn't feel he … deserved it. 'Funny thing, I wasn't afraid, in that crater. One doesn't want to die, of course. But one gets in a certain frame of mind. One pulls oneself together, and gets on with the matter at hand.' He couldn't quite bring himself to look at Bill, was only aware of her staying a diplomatic distance from him. He could not allow himself to break down in front of her. 'Big shock for everyone back in Cromer, of course.'

'You have family?' she asked.

'My wife will miss me, that's perfectly natural. But she's a solid woman. Remarkably solid.' He let the words push away the actual images he had of Mary in his mind, which were so much more than words allowed. 'And my boys ...' Here he had to stop, had to wait until he was sure he could use the words that convention allowed and that his emotions wouldn't betray him as he did. 'Well, sons are supposed to move on from their fathers. It's the proper way.'

'Of course.'

'Trouble is, I thought I'd been rescued. It felt rather like a miracle, in fact. But I do have the feeling that, in the end, they're going to put me back. Back in that crater. In time to die. No matter what your friends do. And you see, I'm not ... I'm not ready any more. I've lost the idea of it. That's the trouble with hope. It makes one awfully frightened.' He took a sip from his brandy and came out with a chuckle, rather against his will. 'I must sound like the most dreadful coward.' He felt he'd better change the subject, for decorum's sake.

Bill must be embarrassed as all get-out. He looked up to find her.

There stood the Glass Woman.

As she reached for his face, Archie just had time to cry out.

Doors of iron, raddled with rust, stood open in the crumbled, blackened wall of the tower. Beyond them, the First Doctor could see ancient stone steps leading upward. He had carried his successor this far. The fop seemed to have got some of his strength back.

He disengaged himself. 'Okay, I'd better go up alone.'

'I won't hear of it.'

'The thing up there won't miss the chance to kill me twice.' He pointed between them. 'The paradox would rip the universe apart. And you know how much hard work it is putting it back together again.' The First Doctor was about to agree when he realised he really didn't. 'You keep a lookout down here.'

For a moment the First Doctor wanted to argue, but then he saw the determined, and quite lost, look on the man's face. 'Very well, if you insist,' he tutted. 'If I do see anything, what do I do?'

'Oh, you know, talk a lot, make something up and sound confident.'

'The usual.'

'The usual.' And the Doctor set off into the tower and up the stairs.

The First Doctor looked around apprehensively. He had an inkling what these creatures were that were whispering and gibbering in the shadows all around. And he didn't like that inkling one little bit. His gaze fell on something on the ground, something half concealed in shadow, a familiar shape. Was that what it looked like? He took a tentative step forward to examine it.

The Glass Woman stepped from the box that belonged to the two men who were the same man, and took a moment to sense every detail of her surroundings, from tiny scent traces on the air to infrared remnants of heat presences on the ground.

She could see which way the two who were one had gone. Calmly, she set off after them.

The Doctor was having a hard time with these stairs. Just as well he hadn't brought the other one, it'd have been double the exertion, plus a lot of complaining. He paused for breath. He must be somewhere near the top now. Sure enough, now he could see over the next landing, there was the door to the central room at the summit. From it streamed an ominous light. The Doctor readied himself for a last exertion and made his way towards it.

The First Doctor had squatted to examine what he'd seen. It was a disc, yes, something like a lens. It was obscured by the darkness, a few feet over there in the guttering. He wanted to reach out for it, but he had no idea how close the creatures were. Dare he? Yes, what nonsense, of course he dared! He reached a hand into the shadows.

The Glass Woman looked down at this version of the one who was two, watching him inch his hand towards the darkness. He grabbed hold of whatever he was after, and started to tug at it. She recorded and shared all she was sensing from him. Her approach had been utterly silent, she was pleased to note. Or at any rate he hadn't noticed her arrival.

The Doctor pressed himself against the wall of the tower, and inched closer to the door. His friend must be aware of his arrival. He called towards the opening. 'You know what? You're a bit of a legend these days. Not everyone believes it. People don't think it could happen, that someone like you could turn against your own kind. Because your kind don't do that.' He braced himself, hoped his words had been intriguing enough to ensure his survival, rolled away from the wall and stepped into the doorway. 'Because people don't believe there could be any such thing … as a good Dalek.'

13

Enter Rusty

The First Doctor had pulled his prize from the ooze. He looked at it in grim resignation, now certain he understood what his other self had been hinting at. 'Out of their shells!' he muttered to himself.

In his hands he was holding the broken-off eyestalk of a Dalek.

The Doctor took in what he beheld in the room atop the tower at the centre of the universe. The round chamber was lined with windows, showing the ruins of Villengard under its blood-red sky. Once this had probably been a throne room. Now at its centre lurked a new occupant. The Dalek was ancient, dilapidated. It was connected to various machines in the room, machines that looked like they were keeping it alive.

'Hello, Rusty,' said the Doctor. The nickname he'd once given the Dalek had now become true. This was a Dalek that the Doctor had become unusually intimate with, physically and socially. Miniaturised, he and …

there had been others with him, he was sure, but he couldn't remember their names … they had gone inside this Dalek's casing, right into its brain. The Doctor had forced it to confront certain issues, and had left it hating its own kind. So, the therapy had been useful—for him, and for every other species in the universe, but not necessarily for the Dalek.

'I am not a good Dalek!' it grated at him, furious. '*You* are a good Dalek!' And it fired its blaster.

The Doctor just about managed to jump back, his already damaged coat taking another hit, the lining falling into ashes as he rolled and managed to stumble back to his feet, and out of the room, his back flat to the wall around the corner once again. 'Now, Rusty,' he called through the doorway, 'you know that I'm dying. And if you don't want me to go off and die somewhere else where you can't watch, you've got to stop shooting at me.'

The Dalek paused for a moment. 'I agree to your terms,' it said.

'I'm going to need some proof.'

There was silence for another moment. Then there came the whine of servo motors, the clank of machinery uncoupling. Something was thrown through the door and fell beside his feet with a clang. It was the Dalek's gun stick. The Doctor looked around the door. Where the gun had been there was now just an empty socket in the casing, circuitry sparking inside it. The Dalek could, of course, summon the gun back to itself with a few moments of telekinesis, but those few moments would give the Doctor the chance to exit once again.

The Doctor stepped into the room. 'You know what?' he said. 'You are the very first Dalek that ever got naked for me.'

The First Doctor realised there was someone standing behind him, and jerked around to see who it was. He was relieved that it was Bill. Her presence, he had to confess, was welcome, even if she had been disobedient in leaving the ship. 'Oh, hello, my dear.' He had by now found several pieces of Dalek casing. He stood to show them to her. 'This is very interesting. A lot of Dalek travel machines have been destroyed here. But they appear to have been shot with a Dalek blaster.'

Bill was smiling at him, like she'd finally gotten to grips with the situation, the poor child. 'So you're the first one, yeah? The original version of the Doctor.'

This was hardly the time or place. 'My dear, you should get back to the ship. This place isn't safe.'

'You're the one who stole the TARDIS and ran away.'

'The Captain might be needing you.'

'The Captain's fine. Why did you do it?'

'Oh, I'm sure your Doctor has explained.'

'I'm not even sure he remembers.'

What? Well, that was most disappointing. 'There were many pressing reasons …'

'I don't mean what you ran away *from*. What were you running *to*?'

Excellent! This young woman seemed peculiarly interested in gathering information, but that was an admirable trait in a youth. Perhaps now was indeed a moment that could be used to inform as well as entertain, by sharing some small lessons from his many adventures? 'That is rather a good question!'

'Questions are kind of my thing. How are you on answers?'

'As a matter of fact, a very long time ago, I left Gallifrey to answer a question of my own …'

The Doctor strode around the tower room, making the Dalek turn to follow him, like a particularly gothic and rundown fairground attraction. 'It's been a long time. Remember the good old days? Like when I got miniaturised and climbed around inside you?'

'You taught me to hate the Daleks!'

'Billions of years ago. What have you been up to since then?'

'Destroying Daleks!'

'Yeah, all the ones who come here to murder you. I've seen the mess outside.'

'Why are you here?'

'As a Dalek, you're linked to the Dalek hive mind. All Daleks are. Even those poor things wriggling about outside. Biggest database I know. I'd like to access it.'

It paused for a moment. Dalek incredulity. 'Why would *I* help *you*?'

'Because helping me, in any way, does something wonderful. It hurts the Daleks.'

Another pause. The Doctor was pretty sure he really could hear the cogs whirring. 'Your logic is … ingenious.'

He grinned. 'And just a little bit evil!'

'I approve.'

The Doctor now felt able to approach. He went to the Dalek, and took his sonic sunglasses from his pocket. He tapped them against the Dalek's sucker arm, and heard the sound of vast quantities of information flowing into the creature's cyborg brain. He felt it was about time that Rusty came out with its standard catchphrase about him once again.

'You would make a good Time Lord,' said Rusty.

The Doctor winced. Now *that* was just plain *mean*.

'There is good, and there is evil,' said the First Doctor. He had found the prospect of sharing what he was about to say far too tempting to resist. Especially given that he was on the verge of change, or of death, and surely now was a time when he should feel able to state his reasons, his credo, his origin, you might say. Bill had settled down on some rocks to listen, far enough away from the creatures that he felt they had a moment to talk. 'By any analysis, evil should always win. Good is not a practical survival strategy. It requires loyalty, self-sacrifice, love. So why *does* good prevail? What keeps the balance between good and evil in this appalling universe? Is there some kind of logic? Some mysterious force?'

She was looking at him almost like she knew the answers to his questions. 'I don't know. Is there?'

'I don't know either. But I would like to. Yes. Some day.'

'Perhaps there's just a bloke.'

'A "bloke"?'

'Yeah. Perhaps there's just some bloke, wandering around, putting everything right when it goes wrong.'

Eh? What a strange notion. Did she have anyone specific in mind for this impossible mission? Oh, was she talking about him? Or rather *her* Doctor. This man who had done those terrible things he had seen, had done enough of them to be called a *Doctor of War*. *He* hardly fitted the definition of the good force the Doctor had always sought. 'Well, that would be a nice story, wouldn't it?'

'That would be the best.'

'But the real world is not a fairy tale!'

'You dash around the universe, trying to figure out what's holding it all together, and you really, really, don't know?'

Perhaps it made sense that, as the companion of his successor, she knew something about all this. He had been unable to understand the great equation of ethics in the universe when viewing other races distantly, from Gallifrey, but perhaps he was now going to hear that he had been right to leave, that his later selves had indeed answered that question. 'You know me in the future. Will I ever understand?'

'No, I really don't think you do. Everyone who ever meets you does. You're the only person you know who doesn't understand perfectly.'

He was about to say that he had no idea what she was hinting at, that she should really learn to express herself more clearly, when she got to her feet, stepped forward and ... oh dear, she was hugging him. Yes, well, this display of emotion was perhaps welcome, in the circumstances, but even so ...

'You're amazing, Doctor. Never forget that. Never, ever.'

'Well, that's ... that's very kind of you ...' He looked at the arms that had embraced him, wondering how to most gently disengage himself.

'We just needed to understand you, Doctor.'

Eh? What 'we' was she referring to?

'We should have trusted you from the start.'

Her voice had changed, become much more certain, much more distant and analytical. The First Doctor realised, with a start, that the arms that had enfolded him were no longer clothed in garments, but were … transparent.

The First Doctor stepped back and found himself looking at the Glass Woman.

14

A Whirlpool in Time

Rusty had projected an image into the air in front of the Doctor. It was a woman's face. She was obviously the model for the Glass Woman, and she looked just as calm, just as serene, but this was a real person, of flesh and blood.

The Doctor leaned in to read the accompanying text, in Dalek, ignoring all the swearwords about inferior species.

'Professor Helen Clay, University of New Earth, year five billion and twelve. There's footage. Can you run it?'

The First Doctor was staring, stiff with anger, at the Glass Woman. Her posture was now authoritative, commanding. Had she somehow meant those words when she had disguised herself as Bill? Or had this been a ruse to gain his trust? If so, why then break that trust? Or, oh dear, had he already shared the information she had sought?

'Where is the Doctor?' she asked. Her voice remained calm as ever.

'A spy!' he muttered. 'A spy in the camp!'

Suddenly, Bill was standing there again. 'No,' she said. 'Not a spy.' Did she really expect him to be taken in by such a meagre charade? 'I'm Bill Potts,' with her voice once again. 'But I'm part of Testimony now. To trust the Doctor, they needed to see you through my eyes.'

The First Doctor took a step back. He had no idea what any of this might mean.

The Doctor had been watching a series of informative images, trying to tune out the furious Dalek commentary that went alongside them about how ripe for conquest the looted memory stacks revealed these primitives to be. That was really a stretch, even for Dalek arrogance, because what he'd been seeing wasn't primitive at all, quite the reverse, in fact. The woman in the picture, Professor Clay, was speaking now, as if giving a lecture.

'The Testimony Foundation combines the resources of time travel with the latest in memory-extraction techniques.' The image switched to showing a glaring white chamber, in which were sitting in rows of elaborate chairs, seemingly entranced, people from many eras of Earth history. There were Roman soldiers, primitive tribespeople, Victorian gentlefolk … and they were all being attended to by the glass creatures.

'The near dead,' the narration continued, 'can be lifted momentarily from their time streams, their memories duplicated, and then their physical selves returned to their moment of their dissolution, without pain, distress, or any recall of the process.' She appeared again, a slight, pleased smile on her face. 'Now the dead can speak again. We can hear the testimony of the past. And, channelled through our glass avatars, they can walk among us again. This is the nearest thing to heaven we can make. This is heaven on New Earth.'

The picture froze. The Doctor didn't want to show the Dalek how hard this news had hit him. On one hand ... it *was* her, it was Bill after all. On the other hand, it wasn't her from the moment when they had parted, or anywhere near that, or if it was, it was because Testimony had allowed her access to only part of her memory. It wasn't her as encountered in life. He could see all of them like that if he wanted to. He could have visited all their graves, read about all their lives. He had never let himself. He loved *meeting* them again. And that was what was being denied him, in his moment of greatest need. Humans had invented their own version of the Matrix on Gallifrey, and it was just as unsatisfying.

'Oh,' he said, empty and happy at the same time, 'it's not an evil plan. I don't really know what to do when it's not an evil plan.' This time, everybody got to live. Actually, this time, it turned out nobody was ever properly going to die. He realised that the image had stopped moving while he'd been deep in thought. 'Why did you stop the playback?' The Dalek didn't reply. He turned to look. 'Rusty?'

A voice came from nearby. 'He didn't stop it. They've frozen time again.' Into the room stepped the First Doctor.

'Who has?'

Then, through the image, stepped a figure. It was the physical form of Professor Helen Clay, as preserved in glass, the Glass Woman herself. The figure morphed in one easy movement into the familiar form of Bill. 'Not everything's evil, Doctor. You're not the only kind one in the universe.'

He hated seeing her now. He hated hating it. 'I knew you weren't real,' he whispered. 'I knew you couldn't be.'

'Oh shut up and don't be stupid,' she teased. 'Of course I'm real. What is anyone supposed to be, except a bunch of memories? These are my memories, so this is me. I'm Bill Potts, and I'm back.'

The Doctor couldn't speak. He had once said that a person was the sum of their memories, a Time Lord even more so. He could not believe … he could not *allow* himself to believe that now. He was not a collection to be filed away and neither was she.

Then she stepped right into his face. 'And so long as I'm here, what the hell do you mean, you're not going to regenerate?'

The Doctor looked furiously at his former self, who looked calmly back. He had indeed told this museum exhibit of a person everything. 'I mean,' he said, '*it's my choice*. It is *always* my choice. There has to be an end, Bill.' He had said it out loud now. This had been his choice since he had recovered inside the TARDIS. He was not going to allow the regeneration. He had decided to die. 'For everyone. Everywhere.'

She pointed in what the Doctor assumed was the direction of the TARDIS, and informed by powers beyond herself, she really should know. 'What about the Captain? You know he has to die at his allotted point in time and space. To correct the error.'

That expression on her face ... he was being taken in by that, but he couldn't help but be, not when she had a point. He was being a hypocrite. He could hardly say that he believed in an ending for all things when he was continuing to facilitate the unnatural continuation of this man's life past the point where this entirely non-hostile and ethical system had ascertained he was destined to die. To do so might be to deny him the survival of his memories, to truly and utterly kill all he was. To do so might also rip the space-time continuum apart and allow the grim reapers to appear for so many more than him. If the Doctor was committed to ending his own life, then his ethics meant he had to take Archie back to where his life would end too.

'I'm so tired of losing people.' He looked again to the First Doctor. He was showing this man his own ending also, it was true, but he would forget this meeting, wouldn't he? He wouldn't be burdened by this moment now, through the rest of his lives, would he? Or was he really going to curse his own life with this decision? That was, assuming that his earliest self was not going to mess this all up by refusing his regeneration after all.

'This was us, you know,' he said to the First Doctor. 'We did this.'

'How so?'

'You and me, trying to die at the same time in the same timeline. Our lives are woven throughout time and space. We must have given history an embolism. We caused the timeline error, that put the Captain in the wrong place. We created a whirlpool in time, and landed him at our feet.'

'But why him?' The First Doctor tapped his own chin with a finger. He had, after all, come upon an idea that hadn't occurred to the Doctor. 'What's he got to do with us? What's so important about one Captain?'

The Doctor didn't know. 'Everybody's important to somebody,' he muttered. 'Somewhere.' He was aware that sometimes, mysteriously, meaning and connection seemed to be born from the random interaction of physical processes in the universe. There was sometimes passion hidden within coincidence. The Doctor had never believed that more than when he'd been young.

That sense of the impossible possible was something he had lost. That … *hope* … was something he had lost.

He went to the window and stared out at the destroyed world. If he was going to die, he was going to settle his affairs first. He would not let someone else bear this burden. Besides, wasn't there a tiny question here to settle, the flame of a riddle kindled by the old man? No, that was a thought of hope, and he had none of that left in him.

The Doctor turned back to the Glass Woman who was also Bill. 'If the Captain has to die … one request. This was our fault. Let *us* take him back.'

Bill looked aside for a moment, consulting a greater authority. Which once again indicated, painfully, hopefully, that she was separate from what she was consulting. She looked back to him. 'Agreed.'

The Doctor marched back to the TARDIS, only to find that there were two of them standing there now, his own beside the First Doctor's. He barely looked at those who walked with him. He had nothing to fear from the creatures, now the landscape around him was frozen. He had only to fear the terrible duty ahead.

Then he could die. Then he could rest.

He went into the First Doctor's TARDIS. The Captain had brushed down his uniform, and stood with a look of duty and acceptance on his face.

'Well, then,' said the Doctor. In the early days of this regeneration, he would have been so direct about this, so blunt. He could not bring himself to be like that now.

'Indeed,' said Archie. He must have realised a lot from the Doctor's own expression. 'Time to die.'

15

The Hopes and Fears of All the Years

The Doctor and Archie went into the Doctor's TARDIS. They took off into the Time Vortex. They had left the Glass Woman, still looking like Bill, standing there, watching the TARDIS dissolve. She intended to travel with the First Doctor who, it seemed, had become her confidante, without his future self benefitting from their conversation. The Doctor was sure that, in any case, she could follow them offhandedly wherever they went. Besides, he wasn't lying: there was no clever trick here, he was going to do what he'd said he'd do. As he worked the controls, he was terribly aware of the Captain standing nearby, keeping his courage up, watching with calm interest rather than allowing himself to think too much.

The Doctor looked to the scanner, where the First Doctor was standing beside his own console, looking rather petulant. 'Your TARDIS is slaved to mine,' said the Doctor. 'You'll follow directly behind me.'

'Oh,' he tutted, 'so I'll just get towed along behind, like some sort of—'

The Doctor flipped the mute switch as he continued. He dared to look at the Captain. 'Are you all right?'

'Oh, fine,' said Archie, which the Doctor thought was the most English thing he had ever heard. 'Yes, absolutely. Just thinking. I told the wife I'd be home for Christmas.' He had a fixed smile on his face, determined not to be anything less than stoic. 'Funny how things work out.'

The Doctor managed a sympathetic smile. He hated this. He hated his hypocrisy at hating this, hated that he was being selfish, hated that he had made it his duty to do this, hated himself, hated time and the world, hated … wait. What had the man just said?

Hope suddenly blossomed into the Doctor's mind. Real hope. The thought he'd just had was like seeing a light in the darkness, a gift that had been given to him, to save him, right at the end. Perhaps there was a clever trick still to be played … if it was even possible.

He hit a control. The wrong control. Then he stepped away from the console, walked aside, as if he'd just done that by accident. Why would the universe allow this? No, no! It was impossible. It wouldn't be allowed.

Would it?

The sound of hope came to a terrible place on what had been a terrible day. It came twice. It sang to itself. With a wheezing, groaning, sound, two police boxes appeared side by side on the battlefield.

After a moment, the doors opened, and the Doctors, the Glass Woman and the Captain stepped out onto the frozen, in all senses, mud of the First World War trenches.

The Captain looked around, as if to make sure they'd brought him to the right place, then adjusted his tie, and nodded. 'I suppose …' He stopped himself, but then it seemed that he had no choice but to continue. 'I suppose there's absolutely no way out of this, is there?'

The Doctor did not want to give the man false hope. He desperately wanted to look to the Glass Woman, to make sure she wasn't reacting, to make sure that she wasn't aware that something was amiss. She might intercede at any moment. He could not let his words trip him up now. 'I'm sorry, Captain. Time has to resume its course. For all of us. This is where you're supposed to be. You won't even remember the interruption.'

'I see,' the Captain nodded. 'Jolly good. Just checking.'

The Doctor looked to the First Doctor. This must be agony for him. He had an angry look on his face, but it was anger directed inwards, helpless. He knew that history couldn't be changed, not one line. But still, doing this was just the sort of thing a 'War Doctor' might do. He put a comforting hand on the Captain's arm. 'I regret, Captain, that the universe generally fails to be a … fairy tale, hmm?'

They found the crater. The Captain actually provided them with directions. The Doctor found himself internally counting seconds as he helped the poor man back to what was meant to be his final resting place. The crater, he noted, came complete with handsome German soldier frozen in time on the other side, still pointing his gun.

The Captain found his place, made some calculation about precisely what his posture should be, his gun aimed directly at his opposite number, then looked stiffly up the Doctor and the Glass Woman. 'Right,' he said. 'Thank you. Thank you all.' He was determined, it seemed, to be courteous even to the being who had decreed that his time was up. 'You've all been most gracious in the … unfortunate circumstances.'

The Doctor smiled down at that gloriously enormous euphemism. *Homo sapiens*, eh? Can't live with them, can't die without them.

'I'm only sorry we can't help you more,' said the First Doctor.

'When time resumes, you will not remember this,' said the Glass Woman to the Captain, with all the kindness she could muster. At least she wasn't doing this as Bill. 'A perception filter will also render us invisible.'

'Yes,' noted the Captain, with quite some *sang-froid*, 'one imagines some of those words were attached to actual meanings of some sort.'

'I wouldn't worry about it,' said the Doctor, half-hoping his tone conveyed something more than his words did, but only to his target audience.

Of course, it did not. 'One thing you could possibly do for me, if you were very kind?'

'Oh, anything,' said the First Doctor. 'Name it, young man.'

'My family. Perhaps you could … look in on them, from time to time?'

'We should be delighted,' said the First Doctor, perhaps in the vague hope he'd remember enough about this to actually follow through. The old man looked to him, and the Doctor realised his former self knew full well that he was hoping to save the Doctor's life with another obligation. Well, we shall see about that. The old codger turned back to the soldier. 'What's the name?'

'Lethbridge-Stewart,' said the Captain. 'I'm Captain Archibald Hamish Lethbridge-Stewart.'

Oh. The Doctor almost laughed. Almost. He could feel the universe tying one of its intricate knots around him, but was it a knot for him to grab hold of and climb to safety, or a knot around his neck? Funny thing, destiny. Funny thing, hope. To be offered the name of his dearest friend, Brigadier Alistair Lethbridge-Stewart, to be meeting his ancestor, his … grandfather, at a moment like this. Right at the end? Possibly, still possibly for them both. This was the poetic connection, this particular grandfather paradox, the meaning beyond all physics that had brought Archie to the spot where Doctors came to die.

'I shall make it my business,' said the First Doctor, looking meaningfully at his older self again.

But no, old man, no. He had already made it his business; he had looked after this man's descendants across generations. 'You can trust him on that, Captain Lethbridge-Stewart,' he said gently.

'Thank you,' said Archie. 'Thank you so much.' He took a breath and then nodded. 'I believe I am now ready.'

The Glass Woman didn't even move. She just sparkled. And then, suddenly, the sound and fury of the battlefield was upon them once more. Time had rushed in to claim its own. There was even the sound of a descending shell, right overhead. The Doctor looked to his hands, knowing that to Archie, he was invisible. 'Don't fear that,' said the Glass Woman, noticing his sudden concern.

The Doctor looked to Archie, and saw the bravery on the man's face vanish in a moment, to be replaced by sudden mortal fear. The man opposite him jerked into life too. The men were pointing their pistols at each other, more tense every moment, about to fire. The noise of the descending shell turned into the dull thump of a dud landing nearby. The sound made both men react, made them both twitch, their fingers tightening on the triggers. The Doctor made himself watch. What happened next would tell him if he had made a terrible error – his last error – or if there was still hope.

Archie woke, as if from a dream, as if from some sort of terrible fugue. A sudden sound had jerked him back to reality, he realised. A dud had landed nearby. For a moment there, it had seemed like his fear had been replaced with ... wonderful adventures ... that he could not now grasp or recall. It was as if something beyond the horrors, a fairy tale, had soothed his brow, just for a moment. 'Right,' he muttered, 'where were we? Oh yes.'

There was the gun. There was the German soldier, pointing it at him. '*Bitte*,' said the German, '*das ist verrückt! Ich will dir nicht wehtun!*'

'Cold, isn't it?' said Archie in response. He wished desperately that the man would either kill him or not kill him. 'It's about to get colder, I suppose, for one of us.' Because he wasn't going to be saved, was he? Somehow he knew that he was about to die, was *meant* to die.

The gun was shuddering so much in the German's hands. He was going to save himself, wasn't he? He was going to save himself by killing Archie.

The First Doctor turned away. 'I'm sorry, I cannot. I cannot be witness to this!'

The Doctor grabbed his arm. He hoped his tone would convey the hope that he felt. And damn it, that it was now too late for the Glass Woman to do anything, even if she caught on. 'Watch!'

'We know what's going to happen,' said the First Doctor, helplessly, wondering.

'No. We know what's *supposed* to happen.' He let a little smile creep onto his face. 'When has that ever stopped us?'

The Glass Woman realised something was going on. She stepped closer to them, probably thinking he was about to try something, not thinking, hopefully, that he already had. 'This is where the Captain dies,' she said. 'History cannot be changed.'

'Yeah, people say that to me a lot,' the Doctor said, nodding to the First Doctor, who had a look of sudden possibility on his face. 'By the way, on the way over, I may have interfered with your temporal mechanics, just a little.'

'What have you done?' whispered the First Doctor.

'Nothing much. Just moved everything forward about an hour.'

'That will not change the outcome,' said the Glass Woman.

'Not normally, no,' said the Doctor. 'Not on any other day. But this is 1914.' And now he allowed himself a grin, in the face of death. 'This is Christmas.'

And faintly on the wind, he actually heard it, the sound he'd been waiting for. Yes, and a sudden lack of sound with it, that allowed it. The big guns had stopped firing. The thunder had ceased, while they were talking. The sound that had started while he had caught the Glass Woman's attention was the sound of the greatest hope of all.

It was the sound of enemies singing together.

Archie wondered what this new dream might be. A dream in which the war had suddenly ceased. It was a bit like that dream, that fairy tale, that he couldn't quite remember. The German opposite him had clearly heard it too. He was looking around, lowering his gun. Oh dear God, had peace been declared? Was the war over, just in time? Or was it just …?

'I say,' Archie called to the German. 'Is that singing? Is that … Christmas carols?' Yes, it was, it was 'Silent Night'! 'You know, I could swear it's coming from …' Because yes, the songs were the same, but from different directions, in different languages. 'From both sides!'

The Doctor stepped forward, looking down into the crater, at where the German soldier had lowered his weapon, at where Archie, unaware of the Doctor, was starting, shivering, to clamber to his feet. He looked up to the fields beyond, to where the songs rang across the miles. 'If I've got my timings right, and clearly I have, we should be right at the beginning.'

'Of what?' asked the Glass Woman. He hoped she'd continue to have a fine appreciation of the weave of established history, and of the neat little stitch in time he had just made, to save not nine, but hopefully these two at least.

'The Christmas Armistice!' shouted the Doctor. 'When they all just stopped fighting! When everybody just *stopped*! Because it was Christmas. Christmas 1914. When the human miracle is about to happen.' All around them, soldiers from both sides were climbing from their trenches, advancing into No Man's Land, waving white flags and offering bottles, starting to meet in the middle, to shake hands, to embrace and start to laugh in sheer, giddy relief.

The Captain hauled himself out of the crater and stood beside the Doctor, oblivious, calling out to the soldiers of both sides and pointing down into the crater. 'Excuse me! Hello! Wounded man here!' He took out his whistle and started blowing on it. 'Wounded man!' Stretcher parties from both sides started to make their way over.

'It never happened again,' said the Doctor, turning back to the Glass Woman. 'Not in any war, anywhere. But for a few hours, one Christmas Day, a very long time ago, everybody just put down their weapons, and started to sing.' And he recalled his own battlefield, of only a few hours ago, a battle it felt like he had never left. 'Everybody just stopped. Everyone was just … kind.'

Archie had helped the German soldier out of the crater, and was aiding him now to stumble towards his comrades, as if the whole deliberate slaughter were a road accident everyone was helping with. What a fantasy. What a fairy tale. Lives saved by a story, by songs.

'You've saved him!' chuckled the First Doctor, at once delighted for Archie and tickled by the Doctor's naughtiness.

'Both of them,' said the Doctor, glancing at the Glass Woman, who was indeed letting them go. 'Never hurts. A couple fewer dead people on the battlefield.'

The First Doctor became suddenly serious, stood straighter, seemed to be looking at him now with a new respect. 'So that's what it means,' he said, 'to be a Doctor of War.' And he smiled in appreciation of what his future self was capable of.

It was a generous interpretation. But wasn't today *about* generous interpretations? The Doctor smiled at his old self. 'You *were* right, you know. The universe generally fails to be a fairy tale.' He put an arm around the old boy, and, pleasingly, he accepted it. 'But that's where we come in.'

And around them, as the Glass Woman looked on, accepting ... the battlefield became a celebration.

16

The Long Way Round

The Doctors, their footsteps dogged by the Glass Woman, spent the best part of a day wandering the sights of the former battlefield, unobserved. Every now and then they would stop, and have to deal with their mutual pain, the doom that was still rushing towards them, but then they would rally. The hope all around them kept them going. They talked at great length, about old friends and foes and things yet to come, for one of them at least. The Glass Woman watched and recorded, and never decided to be Bill – or to let Bill speak for herself, whichever it was – which was perhaps for the best, because the Doctor still didn't know what he thought about that.

At the setting of the sun, the Doctors found themselves on a small hill above the lines, watching the troops play an improvised football match. Along the way they had found sweet tea in army mugs, with a dash of whiskey in there somewhere, and decided that there was enough for them to share. They stood there and drank it together. In the distance, some other soldiers were singing 'Auld Lang Syne'. The Doctor recalled that a friend of his who'd compiled a collection of fairy tales in the Scottish language had begun each one with 'in the days of auld lang syne', meaning what was old a long time ago, or 'once upon a time'.

The First Doctor was looking at the setting sun, at the long shadows it cast. '"Oh, look, it's dark,"' he quoted. '"My day is done".'

The Doctor recognised the poem. '"The moon so cold was once the sun".'

'"Each longed-for day that comes at last …"'

'"Becomes, too soon, the longed-for past."'

They clinked their mugs together. 'Borusa,' sighed the First Doctor.

'Worst poet ever.'

'Absolutely the worst.' The First Doctor nodded to the battlefield. 'Remarkable, isn't it? Truly remarkable.'

'Tomorrow they'll all be fighting again, of course.'

'And it seems there will be no more Christmas truces.'

The Doctor didn't want to tell him that the following year there were attempts, attempts which were cruelly stamped out, that there had been executions about Christmas. His eyes sought out Archie, somewhere safe out there, but he could no longer find him. He looked to the Glass Woman. 'But it happened, that's the point. This, all of this, actually happened.'

She inclined her head. It was fixed now. He had been allowed his final stitch. Then she turned, and gestured to nearby, where stood the First Doctor's TARDIS, and his own.

'I think, Doctor,' said the First Doctor, 'it is time we returned to *our* battle.'

The Doctor felt fear grip him once more. 'You really think so?'

The First Doctor grasped his own lapels. 'The good fight must go on. It never stops. No. So, we cannot stop either. Can we?' It was a pointed question.

The Doctor didn't feel up to answering it. Instead, he grimly shook the man's hand. The power of their contact flared energy between them, flared the flame on their palms again. They both had to take a step back. They had done their damage to the timelines. It had been good damage. It had been poetry. But they must not insult that moment of grace by pushing their luck.

'You haven't decided yet, have you?' the First Doctor said.

'I can't do this for ever. There has to be an end.'

'But does it have to be today?'

'Why not? Why not right here, at the only war that ever turned into a Christmas party? I could do worse.'

'Why do you think the TARDIS brought you to *me*, hmm?'

At least he'd finally gotten on board with the idea that she could do that. But the Doctor had to grudgingly admit he might have a point. She had, after all, risked universal disaster to unite them. She couldn't have known that instead she'd get universal justice. 'No idea.'

'Perhaps it was so I could set you an example.'

'A what?'

'Hold tight to what you believe and jump into the dark. Isn't *that* what you said?'

'*You're* going to change, then?'

'Yes. Yes, I think I am ready now.'

The Doctor allowed himself a smile of relief. So he didn't remember this moment of not wanting to regenerate simply because they had met, and the natural forgetfulness brought on by such meetings had worked its magic on them. The First Doctor was not shortly to cause a cosmic catastrophe that would have made the Doctor's memories of anything beyond his first life a mere fiction.

'But I should like to know,' the old man continued, 'are *you*?'

All the Doctor could give him was a sad smile. 'You'll find out. The long way round.'

The First Doctor raised his nose, in that dinosaur way of his, as if he was about to argue, but then subsided again. His sense of fairness had prevailed. 'Whatever you decide ... good luck. *Doctor*.'

'*Goodbye*. Doctor.'

Honour had been accorded in both directions. There were to be no silly names, right at the end, and no talk of ridiculous warrior titles.

The First Doctor nodded, turned, marched off towards his TARDIS without looking back again. *His* mind had been made up by this whole poetic curlicue, thank goodness. The Doctor could feel the change welling up inside him again, demanding its due. He looked to his palm. There was the fire. He clenched his fist. When he opened it again, the flame was gone. All it would take was a continuing insistence on his part, and then, at some point, the flame would not reappear, the change would disconnect from him, this body and mind would be left alone to die. He would not be collected into the Matrix on Gallifrey as the Glass Woman had collected the denizens of Earth. He would die a more traditional death than any of her subjects, than any stay-at-home Time Lord. It was, in some ways, what his story had always been leading to.

But he'd always had such trouble with endings.

He heard cheers from some distance away. A party of British soldiers were heading back to their trenches, still celebrating. At the rear walked a familiar figure. Ah, there was Captain Archie! The Doctor was pretty sure he would now make it back to Cromer. The figure turned and looked around.

He seemed to see the Doctor. Yes, he had! He was staring at him. As if he impossibly recognised the man he was impossibly seeing, somewhere in the back of his mind. Perhaps the power of the regeneration was starting to interfere with the perception filter. Whatever the explanation, the Doctor wasn't about to argue. He raised his tin mug in a toast. Archie stood to attention and saluted him back. The Doctor smiled at the splendid chap. Then Archie turned and walked off into the gathering dusk.

The noise of a TARDIS launch made the Doctor turn to look. The First Doctor's TARDIS was vanishing. Off back to the Antarctic he went – if the old fool had remembered where the Fast Return Switch was. The Doctor sat on some crates and folded his coat around him. Snow had begun to fall, great flurries of it. Was this an apt place for him to die? He didn't want to be cold as he did it. He was sure his former self would want him to keep warm. On the edge of falling into a sleep from which he might never wake, he heard a voice from behind him. 'You okay?'

It was the voice of Bill.

17

Fear Makes Companions of us All

The First Doctor held on to the console of his TARDIS as it plunged back through the Time Vortex. He could feel the change starting … in that he could feel sensations he had never experienced before and did not understand. He also felt very cold, although his hands were glowing with energy. He hoped that showy nonsense would be over before his young friends saw him. He was pretty sure he was going back to them. 'Well, then,' he said. 'Here we go. The long way round. Hold tight.'

But he couldn't hold on to the console in that moment. His grip failed him and he fell, but only to the floor, so far. He lay there looking up at the intricate design of the white ceiling fittings. He was aware of the time rotor slowing to a stop. He was aware of the TARDIS landing. He was aware of an indeterminate length of time before he heard a key in the lock, and the door opening, and then his young friends Polly and Ben were rushing in. They were fussing and fussing, saying things, in the way his beloved humans did, but he was away now, on his journey, the memories of his last hours informing him and yet also fading. His journey would go on, for such a long time. He would change so much. He had so much to do. He had to change to do it. That was something that would always be true about him.

It was far from being all over.

Okay? The Doctor opened his eyes. *You okay*, was that what Bill—or the thing that said it was Bill—had asked? 'Oh, you know,' he replied at last. 'Basically dying.'

'You don't have to,' she said.

The Doctor thought for a moment, then allowed her a smile. 'How do I look?'

'Scary, handsome genius from space?' She said it just like Bill would, like she was taking the mickey.

'Apart from the obvious.'

'Ready. You look *ready*.'

'To do what?'

'Choose.'

The Doctor nodded. He set down his tin mug for a soldier to find and use. 'Shall we go for one last stroll, Miss Potts?'

She smiled, and he realised it was because he had used her name. He kept doing that. 'Well, it's such a lovely evening.' She took his arm.

They strolled towards the TARDIS together. The battlefield around them was soon to be a battlefield again. The landscape mocked their formal gestures. They mocked it right back. 'Little bit cold,' the Doctor remarked.

'It's winter.'

'Yes, it's winter,' he sighed. 'Definitely winter.'

'Do you know what the hardest thing about knowing you was?'

'My superior intelligence. My dazzling charisma. Oh—my impeccable dress sense.' He waved the tattered remains of his jacket. He hadn't even started on the hair. He was getting a lot of pleasure from treating her as if she were the real thing. It was a comfort he could allow himself, as the end approached. They had reached the TARDIS now.

'Letting you go. Letting go of the Doctor is so, so hard.' She gently disengaged herself from him. 'Isn't it?'

There! That was exactly the insight as if from a great distance that one might expect from an archive, rather than a person! 'You see … that's … that's not the sort of thing the real Bill Potts would say.'

'*I am the real Bill!*' She was actually shouting now. 'A life is just … memories! I'm *all* "her" memories! So … *I'm her!*'

'If you say so.'

Bill Potts found herself glaring at the Doctor in mounting frustration. She had been allowed the complete memories of her life back at the moment

Professor Clay had decided she was happy with the Doctor knowing all about Testimony. There had been profuse apologies. Testimony was always, *always*, kind. That limitation had only been placed on her because they'd wanted her reactions from the time she'd known the Doctor, wanted to know who he really was, not what she'd made him in hindsight. She now recalled every Christmas with Heather, every birthday, the cats they'd owned, the decision to live by the sea, the decision to grow old as humans, the moment she, on her deathbed, had told Heather to go back to the stars and be free of these old bodies once again. She'd recalled the last kiss, and the whisper of water against her face, and that she had never seen Heather leave, because Heather had waited until after hope. And here was this man, this stupid, brilliant old and young man, denying her something she didn't just believe, but *knew*, her own personhood. Her little immortality. More than that, here he was, being stupid enough to consider the luxury of mortality for himself. How could she show him? She had all the powers of Testimony at her command, like they all did. What could she do with that? Who was in here with her?

Oh. Well, all right then. 'Okay,' she said, 'I'm going to prove it to you. I'm going to prove how important memories are. Because I've got a goodbye present for you.'

'Oh, that's nice,' he snarked. 'Will I have to pretend I like it? Because quite honestly, that rug …'

'Oh, come here, you.' She pulled him to her, to shut him up, and kissed him on the cheek. And in that moment she went back to being herself, in the shared world of far away, and gave up this glass body to the willing and actually pretty damn determined friend whose voice she'd found nearby.

'Merry Christmas, Doctor,' said a voice in his ear.

The Doctor stepped back from the entirely different lips that had been kissing his cheek and stared at the face of a … complete stranger! No, this young woman was … familiar. No … no … He had to put a hand to his head as the memories swarmed back into him, transferred skin to skin, the memories of … an entire person, a great friend, a great travelling companion and hero, one he had forgotten! He had remembered her once before, hadn't he? Yes, in trauma, after the battle, and then he had made himself forget again, because forgetting her had seemed so important, for her safety … and now he was looking at her face again, that concern seemed so small and ridiculous. Because this person looking at him was so utterly in charge of her own safety, and also, obviously, gone now too, into the same useful afterlife as Bill. She had faced her raven, in the end but doubtless in a surprising way, with style. She'd probably defeated that raven and found an entirely different one. She was smirking as if she had, anyway. Her face was that familiar beloved mixture of astuteness and concern, and there was, as before, not a straight line anywhere on her. '*Clara!*'

'Hello, you stupid old man,' she said.

'You're back!' He wanted to let her inside his head and show her how much of her was in here now. It was like she was dancing through his neurons. The sound of her voice and the things they'd done together were in so many associations, so many connections to other things that he'd been shying away from lately, because they'd seemed so … dull. They had been dull because they had been without her. To see her again was to see hope. Because, after all, wasn't the lesson of her story, the story he had been without, that there *was* always hope? 'You're in my head. All my memories, they're all back!'

'And don't go forgetting me again, because, quite frankly, that was offensive.'

She smiled once again. And then she was Bill again. 'You see?' she said. 'Memories. Important, right?'

He was about to say yes, yes now he saw. He had been frozen inside, and now these ghosts had given him a chance to thaw. The newly born hope hurt inside him. It seemed to be demanding he go on. He hated it for that. He still couldn't face that.

'I know what you're thinking,' said a new voice. '"Where is he?"' From behind Bill stepped a third ghost of his past. It was Nardole, his former assistant, servant, and, in some ways, jailer. He had a big, let's have a party smile on his full moon of a face. 'Hello, sir.'

'Oh,' said the Doctor in reply, 'you're both here now. How does that work?'

Nardole's face fell.

'We can be everyone,' said Bill. 'We are everyone. All those Glass Women, remember?'

'Yeah, it's good, this, isn't it?' said Nardole, tapping his head. 'I lived happily ever after too, before you ask. Cybermen came back a couple of times, and we were still getting Cybermats every spring when I popped my clogs, but basically, we got it sorted. Seven hundred and twenty-eight years, not bad, I thought. Six wives, two of them at once. Good times. All of them in here with me now. Like me, made of glass when I want to be, or when her upstairs does, made of memories the rest of the time. I got taken by accident. They thought I was human and I was like, "Yeah, go on, be heartless and cruel, send me back," and they gave in. All of me is glass now, look.' He held up a glass hand, then reverted it back to flesh. 'Not just the nipples. Got my hair a bit wrong, though, haven't they? I'm always saying that.'

'You don't *have* any hair,' said Bill. Here they were, interacting like they were ... real. He had to smile at it. He was on the edge of accepting it.

'I have *invisible* hair! Or I'm *supposed* to!'

'You know,' said the Doctor, chipping in, 'when you're already dying, you're entitled to think your day can't get any worse. But here you are.'

'Got a suggestion for you, though,' said Nardole.

'Oh, there's a novelty.'

'Don't die.'

Beside him, Bill nodded.

'Why not?'

'Because, if you do, I think everybody in the universe might just ... go cold.'

The Doctor felt despair and anger flare in him at once. How dare they ask this of him? He pointed to the war. 'Look over there! You know what that is? Peace! Peace on a battlefield! Isn't it beautiful? Can't *I* ever have peace? Can't I rest?'

Bill kept eye contact with him, desperate not to let him go. Selfishly desperate, he thought. 'If ... that's what you want. Okay. Sure. Of course you can.'

'It's your choice,' sighed Nardole.

'Only yours.'

'We understand.'

But in their understanding, in their emotion, they were putting such pressure on him. They knew it, too. They kept wanting him to come back, to realise, to step away from the precipice. They just did not get where he was.

'No,' he whispered. 'No, you don't understand. You're not even really here.' He saw Bill start to protest. He went to her and silenced her with a hand. That wasn't what he meant and she knew it. He wouldn't deny her being any more. 'You're just memories kept in glass. You're done. Completed. You don't have to make this decision ever again. Do you know how many of you I could fill?' He found he was getting angry. Fine. Let them see that. 'I would *shatter* you! My testimony would shatter all of you! A life this long … do you understand what it is? It's a battlefield, bigger than this one. And it's empty. Because everyone else has fallen.'

They remained silent in the face of what he'd said. Bill looked desperately sad. Nardole just shrugged.

'You're right. It's my choice. And I will make it the same way I always do. The same way I do everything. Alone.' He turned to step away, to head for the TARDIS. That would be where he'd die. Or … no, it should be at home, on Earth. One foot in and one foot out. That wouldn't be very elegant, would it? Wait, what was he missing here? What was that hurt inside him, that thing that slowed down his walk, made him want to … He spun on his heel and walked quickly back to where they still stood. He calmed himself. He made himself smile, the warm smile they both deserved. 'Thank you,' he said. 'Thank you *both*.' He squeezed Nardole's hand, just for a moment. It felt like flesh. 'For everything you were to me.'

'Aw,' said Nardole, grinning.

'But what happens now,' he said gently, 'where I *go* now …' Bill was still looking so seriously at him. She was on the edge of tears. 'It *has* to be alone.'

She pulled the Doctor to her and hugged him. He held her. And it was a real hug, with no thought in his head about what it might mean or reveal, because it was far too late for that.

Nardole wrapped his arms around both of them. 'Cuddle,' whispered the odd alien who had meant so much to the Doctor. The Doctor hugged him back.

Bill looked into his eyes one last time. Then she started to fade. So did Nardole. He stepped back and watched them go. At the last moment, at the very last second, Bill managed a smile. A smile of encouragement. A smile of hope.

And then she was gone.

The Doctor stood alone. He felt the pain of his wounds and the weight of the ages. He was so tired. He found the TARDIS key in his pocket, and looked at it. 'Time to leave the battlefield,' he said.

He walked to the TARDIS, unlocked it and got inside.

Without looking back, he closed the door.

18

The Doctor Rises

The Doctor only just managed to get the controls working, but finally he got the ship in motion, the noise of take-off filling the console room. He was going to die in the Vortex, then. Well, the TARDIS would take his body somewhere. None of his business. He looked at the console. The old girl was showing him on the monitor a diagram of all space and time. What, was this meant to be what lay ahead for him to explore? 'Oh, there it is. The silly old universe. The more I save it, the more it needs saving. It's a treadmill.'

He felt so … old. So completed. He had wondered, in this incarnation, about every aspect of himself, about his worth, his beliefs, his meaning in a universe that seemed to have forgotten everything he'd learned and didn't see the need to consult him as it was learning those harsh lessons for itself, over and over. He had lived through that. He had lived out the human life he had always envied. He had put aside the questions of his youth, about the mysterious victories of good over evil, as a conundrum that could never be solved. He had known lasting love, he had found peace, he had died a good death, to save others, already. What more could there be for him to learn? He would not be merely the sum of his memories, something to be collected in the Matrix, he would put a proper full stop at the end of his life, like … well, he'd been about to think 'like humans did', but … but he'd just discovered they didn't do that, hadn't he? He'd just discovered something … new.

This damned universe, mocking him at his moment of greatest fear.

The console room made mechanical noises of the kind he'd gradually accepted as being those of a voice, though he usually put a broad interpretation on what it might be saying. 'Yes,' he called back, 'yes, I know, they'll get it all wrong without me.'

The noises came again. They spoke of more than the people of the universe getting it wrong. They spoke of a memory it turned out he actually now had in his head once again, a memory he'd previously forgotten. He could hear her voice, now the machine had made him think of it.

'Perhaps there's just some bloke,' said the voice of Bill in his memory, 'wandering around, putting everything right when it goes wrong.'

He almost laughed. He almost laughed a laugh so big it nearly brought on the change on its own. Oh. Oh! He had learned another new thing, although really he had already known it. He was such … an idiot. A complete idiot—or at least, an idiot who had been completed by this realisation of his own stupidity. Because he had learned new things, had changed twice, in the space of the last few minutes.

Testimony was a human system. It would not save them all. It would not save them from pain and horror. It would not see where lives did not have to end, where change was possible. It was just something else instead of death. Someone still had to save people. Someone still had to help them. But … not someone who was pleased with the life he had completed.

He was satisfied. He had done the best he could. Change was required, because it always was. 'Well,' he whispered, 'well, I suppose one more lifetime … won't kill anyone.' He felt the light start to play with his hands. He'd released it to do so. 'Except me.'

The sound of the Cloister Bell started to reverberate through the console room. So, this regeneration was going to be another big one, was going to be explosive. He climbed slowly up onto the higher level. He wanted to be closer to his library. 'You wait a moment, Doctor,' he called to the spirit of the future that he could already feel jostling to squeeze into his molecules. There were a few things he wanted to say to whatever old or young pale-skinned man took his place. Because he was one of those stuck-in-a-rut Time Lords who always got basically the same model of body. He wouldn't be ginger, either, with his rotten luck. 'Let's get it right! I've got a few things to say to you.'

He swayed giddily along the deck. The TARDIS did seem to be reacting oddly to his impending change, as if it were already in trouble, but … woo, too late now, that was something for the next guy to worry about.

'Basic stuff first. Never be cruel. Never be cowardly.' He suddenly pointed to the spectre of the future he couldn't see in front of him. 'And never, ever eat pears!' Because that was his personal taste, damn it, that was a quirk born of experience, and he didn't want to squander it. That had been with him since his tenth life, and when that man had become human for a while, what had he done? Eaten all the pears, that's what, and he'd had to wake up from that experience with a mouth full of that. He was suddenly struck with something he really did want to pass on, something that was the product of much longer experience. 'Remember,' he called, 'hate is always foolish, and love …' He let himself recall the long details of his own love for a moment. 'Love is always wise.'

He stumbled back down the stairs from his high and mighty pulpit, back to the console once again. This was where he had lain that first time, wasn't it? He could do worse. 'Always try to be nice,' he hissed through the increasing pain. 'But never fail to be *kind*.'

He stumbled on, straight past the console, hilariously, all the way to the doors, like he was going somewhere. He felt drunk on the energy of renewal, of completion. He spun back and yelled at the room. 'Oh! And! You mustn't tell anyone your name.' His walk took him back towards the floor that awaited him. 'They wouldn't understand it anyway. Except—'

He didn't make it past the console this time. The pain took him and he fell. He lay there for a moment. He was starting to boil. The steam was rising from him. His flesh was in a crucible. Or was that also the smoke from … *was* there something wrong with the TARDIS? He didn't know either way. He hauled himself up. He would finish his sentences. He would end deliberately and consciously. His life's meaning *would* be complete.

'Except for children. Children can hear your name, sometimes. If their hearts are in the right place, and the stars are too.' He thought of the children the future Doctor would meet, those that would be inspired by him, by … them? What was this? Agony seized him again, and he reflexively grabbed the console. 'But nobody else,' he whispered, pulling himself to his feet. 'Nobody else, ever.' This was his house, these were his rules, these were what a man had to hang on to. But he had to let go. Because … oh. Oh yes. He could see someone now. In his mind's eye. He could see the future.

'Laugh hard, run fast,' he said to them. 'Be *kind*.'

He stood there. He adjusted his cuffs. It was all going to be all right. Of course it was. Seeing who he was going to be, he was suddenly filled with ... hope.

'Doctor,' he said, 'I let you go.'

He let the fire take him.

Epilogue

And there the new Doctor was: standing in clothes that were far too big, in uncomfortable boots, looking at the steaming mess that the regeneration process had made of the console. The wedding ring fell from the Doctor's finger. It made a small noise as it fell to the floor of the TARDIS.

Okay, focus on one thing. One thing. Here was the monitor, which was buzzing with static, the image on it flickering. What was it to be this time? There was something different about this body, wasn't there? Facing her was a young woman with a swish of blond hair, astonished eyes and a pleasing, goofy, grin. She stared at her reflection.

'Oh,' she said, 'brilliant!'

Change was possible. Change was here. What had she been worrying about just now? No idea. She hit the first button of a navigation sequence.

The console exploded. Just for a moment, the Doctor saw a warning flash onto the monitor screen.

Systems crisis. Multiple operations failures. Was there actually something wrong with the TARDIS? What had caused this?

She didn't have another moment to think. The TARDIS spun violently, sending her head slamming into the deck. She watched as the gravity went wild, her library shelves falling off the upper deck. She grabbed for the vents in the floor panel and managed to hold on as it went from being a floor to being a vertical wall, with her hanging from it.

Suddenly, the ship's doors burst open. The atmosphere inside the ship flew outward. At least they must be somewhere, not in the Vortex. But she couldn't hold on against this new force grabbing at her coattails. She flew towards the doorway. Her feet hit the edge of it as she desperately flailed to grab hold of something … anything!

At the last second, her fingers grabbed hold. She managed to haul herself back up towards the console as all her books, her papers, all the records of her travels, flew past her, falling into whatever was out there. She managed to get one hand, now both hands, back on the console. She chanced a look back over her shoulder. Okay, okay, all she had to do was—

There came a sound from in front of her. She turned back to look. Fire burst up the central column of the console, cracking it as it went. The tremendous energies of the TARDIS were about to—!

Light and sound erupted into her face and the Doctor flew backwards, like an arrow, towards the door, her flailing hands failing to grab at anything. She fell straight out through it, like one of the billions of pieces of paper that were falling around her. Behind her, through the police box doors, she saw a fireball erupting, consuming everything inside. The light on top of the box began to flash urgently, and the sound of the TARDIS's departure roared before the blast could leap out of it and consume her—consume everything!

The TARDIS vanished.

The Doctor fell, arms cartwheeling. Below her, as she spun, she saw the lights of a city at night.

It was just her now, in this terrifying second. Without a TARDIS. Falling from what must be several thousand feet. Towards a completely unknown destination.

Towards her future.